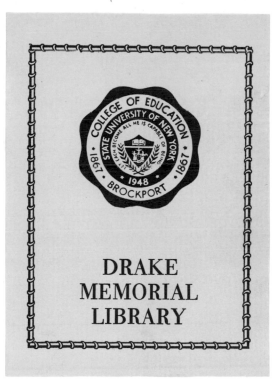

The Maniac Responsible

TO CAROL AND STEVE OLIKER

The Maniac Responsible

by
Robert Gover

Grove Press, Inc. New York

The Maniac Responsible

A Twig in the Stream

The time: 4 A.M.

The place: a cranial cavity abed in one of a set of cubicles in the town of Ridiculee, county of Ridiculeye, state of Depravity, united states of Absurdity, on a rural planet in the vast universe of No Reason.

The event: approximately as follows:

TOO MUCH
SCIENCE
FICTION

I SHOULD
TAKE NOTES

like a japanese garden almost but not like that really really like a zoo because there is this huge hairy beast who eats everything and the guide says it eats constantly and can't get enough so ravishes whatever comes its way just like a storm sewer sucking up rainwater or like a starving man discarding only what he can't digest and it's in this big cage like a building as big as a building and the guide is like a maniac cuban peanut vendor laughing incessantly laughing and moving about with nervous spasms but moving as if bogged down in mud and laughing a fake stagy laugh like for the benefit of those in the balcony but there isn't any balcony and everything seems up close

5

**WHY DO
THEY DO IT**

**IT CAN'T
BE MORNING**

**IMPOSSIBLE!
I JUST FELL
ASLEEP**

to the guide and also close to the cage and the beast so there's something phony about it and maybe it's the keepers yes at least a dozen keepers all in striped suits like convicts working feverishly to keep this grotesque monster fed by dumping all kinds of stuff into a trough like bushels of corn and wheat and truck-loads of garbage and fish and machinery and now and then a man or woman making a great stinking concoction of refuse sliding down the groove of the trough right into the monster's mouth and down his gullet and he seems to take it all in one chew and swallow effortlessly and quickly so that the pouring mixture slides like it was greased from the keepers' ladles down the trough and down into the beast and the stream is unbroken like an electric current but then all of a sudden everything jangles the beast does and his cage and keepers and the guide and the ground and everything else and then after that nothing is the same when the vibrations stop and the scene melts into something indescribable as if blending into a montage to assume its proper place in the scheme of things fuzzy and meandering until it merges and glows and fades and glows again and fades again and the guide's laugh grows softer and softer until finally he's seen and heard as if from a far balcony and can no longer penetrate and has to accept it for the fake it really is and accept reality really.

The phone rang at 4 A.M. Dean had been asleep only an hour. He wasn't completely awake when he said, "Hello." His eyes stayed closed and his head on the pillow.

"Dean," came the urgent voice from the other end of the line, upturning his name into a question, "Get up, boy. This is Scotty and there's a woman in the township with a hatchet in her skull. I just got the word from headquarters this minute. You're the first to know about it, boy, so move!"

LUCKY STRIKE said the pack of cigarettes when he switched on the bedside lamp. He slid one out of the pack with the fingernails of his thumb and forefinger; he dragged it along the tabletop to his lips, squinting in the sudden blinding of the light. "Where?"

"You go out Swamp Run Road past Ziggy's and swing up the first dirt road to your right. It's just a little deadend bit of a road. I don't know the name of it but it's a mile past Krutcher's Corners, just after Ziggy's Pig Farm. Now for God's sake, Dean, don't breathe a word to anybody about this call."

He found a match, struck it on the tabletop, and lit the cigarette. "Don't worry, Scotty, I won't. I'll see you there."

"Yeah. Hey, they tell me it's a red and white cottage, pretty new, first one in on the left. Got it?"

"Yeah. I'll find it. How long ago?"

"I'm telling you, I just this minute got the call from headquarters. You make up some excuse, okay?"

"Yeah, okay."

Scotty hung up with a clunkedeeclunk which hurt his ear. There was that pause when morbid, dream-infested sleep beckoned, then he whipped off the covers, took one foul-tasting, lung-burning drag on the cigarette, and lay exposing himself to the early morning chill until goosebumps rose drawing him up, swinging his legs down, rolling his weight onto his feet, stumble walking to close the window. He stretched and yawned and inspected his image in the dresser mirror—flattened crewcut hair atop the dumb-animal bulldog set of his face, mouth closed on the taste of unfinished sleep, dry and smoke-scratched throat, eyelids threatening to close. Seemingly disconnected feet carried him bumpingly through the bedroom door to the bathroom, and at the sink he decided that since he was at the sink he was up for the day, awake, on his way, but not up enough to endure a shower, so he decided to brush his teeth and let it go at that for now. This he did, GERM KILLING GL 70, GUM STIMULATING, SUPER CLEANSING POWER. Then he felt better, good enough to dash cold water on his face to shock the sleepiness out of himself. This he did, then went back to the bedroom and put on yesterday's shorts and teeshirt, and clean socks, old jeans, a torn sweater, hunting boots, windbreaker. He didn't bother to relight the cigarette.

The door to his apartment faced the door to her apartment and when he stepped into the hall and saw her golden V-shaped knocker he felt the temptation strongly again—to knock, to rouse her, to enter wordlessly and wordlessly without fanfare bridge the gap. As he turned and walked along the hallway toward the stairs to the front door, his need flooded with her image and with the lack of having her, with her appeal and her silliness. She had moved into her apartment a week ago and he had had his first date with her last night; it had lasted until 3 A.M. Now, an hour later, as he walked down the hall, he thought of what he should have told her, and now silently told her: Damn it, Sweet Reet, the least you could do is thumb your nose at me so I could say, yes yes, you delicious darling, your very wish is my command. Thus he chortled to himself of the object of his yearning, of her proximity, her disdain, her tempting, rebuffing, cajoling, withholding, her teasing brinksmanship. His daydream: Soon he would have her, tonight if possible, and on his terms, not hers. It warmed him, this thought did, and momentarily occupied him so fully that he wasn't even aware of the loud thump-tapping of his boots on the hall's hardwood, nor the doors of other apartments as he whisked past them, cutting through the hall's stale air in the early morning stillness.

Down the creaking, rubber-covered stairs and out through the squeaking wooden door of the building he went, then right along the sidewalk beside the stone facade of the apartment building to his battered Super V-8. The loose rattling sound of its door closing him in switched his thoughts to the moment. A streetlight glared him in the eye as he probed with the ignition key; the engine zing-hummed alive and he went whirring away over the blacktopped street to the highway, then on toward that grand abstract absurdity, the political boundary, the town-township line.

SPEED 35 MILES

His mind confronted its image of Scotty's brief message: an old woman with her skull battered, lying in a pool of blood, stiff, dead, like the old woman who had been hit by a train about six months ago.

STOP

He imagined she would be in an old-fashioned silk nightgown, in the kitchen or living room, surrounded by a large pool of blood. She would be a very old and wrinkled woman, living on a pension or social security and kind neighbors or children in one of a cluster of those strange, rundown, flimsy houses in the wilds of the township between the suburbs and the countryside where small farms had once been. Yes, she would be surrounded by blood, he feared, and her shack by a cluster of shacks, and the shacks by wooded hills on one side of twisting Swamp Run Road and on the other side by the stream it followed and the marshes near the stream.

HARRY'S HIDEAWAY   DANCING SATURDAY

Then it occurred to him that he should stop and call for a cameraman, but he sloughed off that thought by telling himself there would be plenty of time for that later, once he had

seen what it was all about, and later the pictures wouldn't be
so bloody.

WELCOME TO KRUTCHER'S CORNERS

STOP

NOW SHOWING: SLAVE MAIDENS AT THE
MERCY OF HIDEOUS BEASTS   ALL NEW   FRIGHTMARE OF
MOVIE MONSTERS   UNSPEAKABLE HORROR   GHOULS CAP-
TURE GIRLS   LIVE FROM AUDIENCE   GIRLS, BRING AN ES-
CORT TO PROTECT YOU WHEN THE LIGHTS GO OUT   DON'T
DARE COME ALONE   SEE BEAUTIFUL GIRLS TORTURED BY
MONSTERS

Ah, he thought, maybe he would take Rita to see that movie
tonight; maybe that would loosen her up some. On the other
hand, maybe that movie would put him in such a foul mood
it would do no good to have her loosened up. Oh well. The
city papers will ride this thing hard, he told himself, switching
back to the murder. But I'll beat that with an eyewitness sidebar, or something. Hey! Where the hell's the nearest telephone? Must remember to call a photographer right away,
must remember that. Mustn't let my mental blocks work
against the advertising department. Woman with a hatchet in
her skull. *In* her skull? Did Scotty mean it was still *in* her
skull? Aw. Impossible. Besides, how would he know? Just got
the call himself. No, it couldn't be still in her skull. If she's
an old woman, it won't be so noisy; but what if she turns out
to be young?

WOULD YOU LIKE A BARBEQUED HAM FREE?
FOLLOW THE GREEN ARROW TO
ZIGGY'S PIG FARM.

He wheeled right off the concrete highway onto the blacktopped, humpbacked Swamp Run Road and straddled the
hump with the wheels.

SPEED 35 MILES

OH DARLING   YOU REMEMBERED

DANGEROUS INTERSECTION AHEAD

GET THE CAR WITH THE GO

STOP

He probably could have waited until later to go out, he thought as he tracked along the winding, two-lane byway, especially since he wouldn't get paid for this overtime. Later he could have gotten all the bloody details from Scotty, or Chief John, maybe. And if he had stayed in bed he wouldn't be obliged to concoct one of those hatefully corny, fantastic eyewitness accounts. Lord knows I need the sleep, he told himself, but if you can jump the gun, you do, whether you feel like it or not. Force of habit. Even if it's for some story hardly anybody will read. And for some entertaining horror like this one—man, you go like a jackrabbit. You run for it, he observed with clenched teeth as he swung too fast into a sharp curve, laughing at yourself as you run.

The happy treadmill, Ally.

The inky go-round, comrade.

One of these days he should, he decided, hunt for a public relations job with no game of tit for tat with police and politicians, no 4 A.M. jaunts after an hour's sleep because somebody put a hatchet into somebody's skull—no guff from hobby cops who know all about newspaper guys from the TV shows, no pressured editor pressuring you to dish up puerile gore on an honorable, active verb to that insatiable beast, no listening to the ravings of a preacher disquieted by a squib of a sodomy story.

FIDELITY SERVES YOU

SLOW MEN WORKING

HAPPY'S BAR AND GRILL   DINE AND DANCE

DANGEROUS CURVE SLOW

LIVE BETTER BY FAR
IN A BRAND NEW CAR

SLOW SCHOOL

SPECIAL SALE   KITES, BALLOONS REDUCED

Seems everybody has to please some monster these days in order to make it, he mused. I please Scotty by running, he pleases me by calling. By running when he calls, I please Brady, who pleases Johnson with, we hope, a better story than the city papers, a gorier, storier story, because that's how just plain folks like them, which makes everybody so bloody happy, including Reverend Iseman because it gives him a chance to come into the office and loosen up his righteousness at me and shout his loud pieties. *Poof* goes his steam!

ZIGGY'S PIG MARKET AHEAD

He switched on the car radio. It sang:

Go go go, little tweedy

He kept driving, watching for the dirt road now.

PREPARE TO MEET THY GOD

BUY A PIG FROM ZIG
SLAUGHTERING DONE
SAVE   SAVE   SAVE

JESUS SAVES

It looked more like a driveway than a road. He couldn't have missed it if he'd tried. A police car spotlight was trained on the front of the house; it drew his eye from the road. He glided the car to a stop on the road's shoulder just past the lane up the small embankment to the scene. He leaned over to the glove compartment, yawned, took out a notepad, leaned back, pulled a pencil from a clip behind the sunvisor and emerged from the car thrusting forward toward the spot-lit house. The cinder-covered mud lane was squishy under foot. He was glad he had worn the boots. It was only a short distance up the lane to the cottage but it took twice as many steps to walk it because of the mushy underfooting.

The house was a one-story, newly painted, neatly land-scaped place: that much was evident. He couldn't see its color and size because of the spotlight's intensity and limitations, and because of a mist rising from the stream on the other side of the road. The mist and spotlight, each lending its own aspect to the fresh paint of the shingled cottage, created a rare effect—grotesque brightness shrouded. Behind the police car, standing in the fog and darkness, were people from the semicircle of homes in the little community, barely visible in the haphazard illumination from lights in windows. Men, women and children—hastily dressed, hands in pockets or folded over chests against the spring morning's chill dampness—seemed dumbfounded, motionless, expectant. They stood stiffly, as if ordered from their homes by some familiar enemy, watching the front of the spotlit cottage intently, awaiting further orders.

He took in the scene as he trudged up the cinder-over-mud lane. He noticed that the people numbered about twenty-five, that the spotlight came from a township police car, and that no one stood on the cottage's front porch or in its doorway. He hesitated a moment between the silent huddle of people and the steps to the porch, then walked up the steps to the porch and in through the open door. From the darkness inside the door came hands and a loud voice: the hands twisted his right arm behind him and held his hand tucked up between his shoulder blades, and the voice shrilled, "Hey, where the hell you think you're going? Who are you, anyway? Come on, make it good."

He winced at the sudden pain inflicted—he knew immediately—by some hysterical part-time agent of law and order, then when the other ended his questions, he replied,

"I'm the killer, returning to the scene, you jackass. Now let the arm go or I'll sink a hatchet in your skull."

"Hey, Chief!" yelled his captor. "Got a wise guy here. What should I do with him?"

A voice Dean recognized as belonging to the chief of the township police responded. "Who is he?" It came from the cellar.

"Some kind of nut, I guess."

There was a period of silence punctuated by the scuff and clomp of shoes on wooden stairs, then a door opened and the flashlight-bearing chief entered the kitchen from a door to the cellar. Dean was blinded as the flashlight searched his face.

"Ha! Dean! He's all right, McCarthy. Works for the paper."

McCarthy, an enthusiast, gave Dean's arm one last twist, then released his grip. "He's still a wise guy. Said he was the killer. Guy says that, he deserves whatever he gets. Better watch it, young fella. This is no laughing—"

Dean cut McCarthy short with a question to the chief. "Is the county here yet?"

"Scotty just got here. The rest are on their way. Pretty horrible down there. Never seen anything like it."

"Mind if I take a look?"

"Sure, it's okay with me, if you can stand it. But I'm warning you, it's pretty awful. Don't touch anything," said the chief, leading the way. "Fingerprints. That's why the lights are out. Never can tell where fingerprints might be. Buzzed the deputy coroner, too. He'll be out in a minute."

Dean snickered to himself at the chief's sudden importance as he followed the beam of his flashlight down the cellar stairs, glancing back for a quick look at McCarthy—a bundle of silent grumbles—silhouetted in the front doorway by the police car spotlight. About halfway down the stairs, Dean halted and stared. In the center of the cellar's bleak concrete floor, under one bare, dim light bulb hung from an extension cord, lay the woman. She was neither old nor in a pool of blood. She was, Dean's senses screamed, in her twenties. The top of her skull had been bashed; under her matted hair it looked as if it had been erupted by an internal explosion which had left her face intact. The blade of the hatchet was buried in the top of her head, left by its user as if in a chopping block. Her blood lay in smears and puddles on either side of her. She lay on her back staring up at him with eyes and mouth wide open, as if shocked to find him finding her. Her housecoat had been spread open and her panties and bra torn loose, exposing her from the neck down. Her bare body seemed fresh and young, and separate from the shocked and shocking face; it lay white and delicate against the gray floor under the light, something remote and of beauty, with a triangular patch of pubic hair at its center. Inside him, an ebb and swell of unstoppable emotion at the sight of her helpless, vulnerable flesh against the gray cement floor rose and receded; the unthinkable screamed its frightening scream from deep in its subchamber, and was promptly muffled, even before it had been consciously heard.

He lit a cigarette, huffed a sigh of smoke toward the pink and white glowing female flesh, and continued his descent, stopped only once more by a vague impression which tumbled through him like a forgotten melody: an image of the rape and murder fleetingly enacted, and the whispered, cloudy sensation of knowing more than he cared to admit knowing of what it had been like. This image was, he quickly told himself, not a thing to be imagined, or even thought of. He shuddered, trying to deny it, but it persisted like the after-effects of a compulsive act, until he heard Scotty's voice.

"Hello, Dean. What are you doing here so quick?"

"Somebody called. One of the neighbors. They want all the dope, you know. All the details."

Scotty stood in the cellar looking up at him from the other side of the body. "Yeah, that's right. But do me a favor and stay there on the steps, will you. And John, tell your guy at the door no unnecessary spectators. God knows this place will be overrun soon enough."

"Sure," said John, turning to go quickly past Dean and up the stairs, leaving Dean alone with Scotty and the wide-eyed, open-mouthed, bare-bodied woman. Dean felt his knees trembling; he sat down on the third step from the bottom. Then, trying to recover, he checked his wrist watch and noted the time—4:43—on his notepad. He felt awkward using a notepad instead of the usual sheaf of copypaper, awkward at the foot of the woman's motionless, inverted V, awkward in the thick silence of Scotty's company. He felt released when John clomped his way back down the wooden stairs and stood, stern-masked, yet retaining in his oval face a hint of jack-o'-lantern joviality, legs militantly spread, hands clasped behind his back, as if awaiting further commands from note-taking Scotty. John's manner reminded Dean of a schoolboy traffic patrolman; Scotty's of a pacing caged animal on display —pleasant on the surface but hiding a dangerous restlessness. Scotty seemed so absorbed in his work and John so unoccupied that Dean, to fill the vacuum, asked John, "What time'd the call come in?"

"Mmm, about three-thirty. Yeah, three-thirty. Next-door neighbor—name's Herder—noticed the cellar door open. He's a milkman, Herder. Looked in that window over there, saw something wrong, came in and found her."

Then Dean's questioning was nipped at its beginning by the arrival of the deputy coroner, bumping down the stairs in heavy mill shoes and old work clothes; he had just been called away from his regular job in the local steel mill. He brushed Dean's shoulder with his knee as he passed, then went shuffling indolently over to the corpse. He stood a few seconds staring down at the dead woman. Then he cast Dean a scowl and kneeled down beside one of her legs and lowered his head until it almost touched the floor between her knees, and inspected her vagina. He remained in this position for about half a minute, with Dean and John watching him, then he straightened stiffly, dusted off his trouser knees with his hands, shook his head, made a few clucking sounds with his tongue and lit a cigar.

The deputy coroner's was a job of political patronage, his activities pure ritual; he could do nothing official until a doctor arrived. His clucking sounds reminded Dean that soon the house would be crawling with detectives, reporters, photographers and the card-carrying curious, and that he no longer had any excuse for not calling a cameraman. He stood, stretched, turned and scuffed up the wooden stairs to find a telephone.

Dawn was attempting to pierce the haze and darkness now; it dimmed the spotlight and made the fog an all-pervading veil. He could see the vague outlines of furniture inside the cottage —the kitchen painted bright yellow with red trim, a large refrigerator-freezer, an electric range. He saw that the living room and kitchen were separated by a stone planter overflowing with ivy and that the pieces of furniture in the living room were too large for the size of the room—a long, custom-made leather couch, a television-phonograph console, a leather easy chair and large tables, with little floor space left. He ignored McCarthy's intent gaze and found the phone on the wall near the end of the planter, but when he reached for it, McCarthy bellowed:

"Don't touch that!"

And Dean's hand shot back reflexively.

"Get away!" shouted McCarthy. "Stand back! Hey, Chief!"

The chief came halfway up the steps. "What?"

"This guy's fooling with the phone."

"That's okay. Prints'd be smeared on it anyhow. Go ahead, Dean, make your call. But don't touch anything else."

Dean gave McCarthy a look of exaggerated snobbishness and picked up the phone. He called Charley Phillips—tranquil, agreeable Charley Phillips, instead of one of the others.

"'Lo?" came Charley's groan.

"Hello. Charley?"

"Yeah."

"Dean."

"Yeah?"

"Yeah. Hey, there's a woman with a hatchet in her skull out in the township." Dean wondered if Scotty had felt as theatrical as he now felt uttering those words.

"What's that? A hatchet?"

"Yeah. Some good shots if you can make it out here fast. First turn past Ziggy's, up a dirt road, just off Swamp Run."

"Yeah?"

"Yeah. About a mile past Krutcher's Corners on Swamp Run."

"What did you say was there?"

"A woman with a hatchet in her skull."

"Oh. Yeah. Well. Okay, I'll be out as soon as I can make it."

"Well, you'd better make it quick, Charley, 'cause they're waiting for the crime lab guys now, don't know how long they'll let her be."

"Hmm. Well. Tallyho," drawled Charley, "I shall make haste."

"Okay. Bye."

"Bye."

Good old Charley, thought Dean as he hung up, making haste. Leaving his warm, chubby wife, getting out of his warm bed, lumbering about his bedroom finding clothes, walking tall and gaunt with a puzzled, vacant expression on his long, sad face, making haste. And if he made haste slowly, so what. He'd been in the news game about twenty years now, pulled from his bed how many times, to go lumbering sad-eyed into the midst of how many madnesses?

Dean turned from the phone and headed for the cellar again, then stopped short. The front door was abuzz with sudden activity—the arrival of half a dozen men from the county crime lab trying to get past McCarthy who had taken command impressively, demanding to see their identification.

McCarthy's chunky form filled the doorway and over his shoulder Dean saw the faces of the detectives and among them, the face of an old reporter who had wisely decided to pose as a detective since he found himself among them and stopped by McCarthy. Dean chuckled to himself at the scene. The reporter was Ed Cory, described by Scotty as "over the hill, punchy, on nightside too long." Cory was shouting repeats of words and phrases the others were using on McCarthy.

"Look, mister, whoever you are, we're from the crime lab and the DA's office. Now one side, please."

"Yeah, one side."

"Out of the way, mister."

"Out of the way."

"Say, what's the holdup, anyhow?"

"Yeah, anyhow."

"No admittance," boomed McCarthy, "except to authorized personnel." He chanted this, rolling the syllables tastily over his gums. "And all authorized personnel must show identification. Chief's orders."

"Chief of what?"

"Yeah, what?"

"Chief John of the township police."

"Jesus Christ."

"Yeah, Jesus Christ."

"What the hell's this guy talking about, identification?"

"Look, Mac, this stuff we're carrying—that's our identification."

"Yeah, that's it."

"You think we're hauling this stuff around for our health?"

"Yeah, do you?"

"Hey, who the hell's this bohunk, anyhow?"

"Yeah, who is he?"

"Look, fella," said the detective at the head of the pack, "I don't know who you are or what you're doing here, but be a good guy and step aside and let us in, okay?"

"I got my orders," said McCarthy.

"He got his orders," shrieked Cory, doubling up with laughter.

"Come on, Mac, let's get the show on the road."

"He got his orders," yelled Cory to those behind him.

Then Chief John appeared from the cellar and gently induced McCarthy to admit them. McCarthy stepped aside, folded his arms over his chest and wrinkled his face into the type of stony mask used by women to conceal hot flashes, and the detectives filed through the door and down the cellar stairs, with Cory among them. Dean took up the rear of the procession.

Now the cellar was full of men and their clouds of cigar and cigarette smoke, and the chants and hums of mumbled conversations and exclamations of horror—all in an aura around the bare body of the woman on the floor. The detectives paused a while to take in the scene, then dispersed to their various tasks—making pictures and molds, collecting tiny things with tweezers, dusting for fingerprints. Dean returned to his place on the third step from the bottom and watched. Cory prowled about boldly, inclining his head, bending, peering at the corpse this way and that, noting the angle of the hatchet handle, the damage to the skull, closely inspecting the dead woman's still fresh and lovely skin, and all the time, Dean observed, straining to hear what the detectives said. After a short time, Cory was joined in his close examination by the deputy coroner—back for a second inspection. The two of them carried on a muted conversation as they went bending and straightening, squatting and rising, around the body like a pair of high priests of some strange cult performing a last-rites dance in slow motion. Dean watched, as if put in a trance by some otherworld hypnotist.

He didn't know how long he was held by the spectacle, but his trance was finally broken by a bit of conversation which came drifting softly up to him from a group of detectives. "Where's the boy now?" someone asked. It made no impression on him at first. But, slowly, he turned his head to the group of detectives huddled around Scotty, and slowly pulled out his notepad to write, *Boy* under *4:43*.

Then, feeling vaguely alarmed by the lonely disconnected items he had noted on the pad since Scotty's 4 A.M. phone call, he rose and ambled carefully over to Scotty's side. When the others moved away again, Dean touched his shoulder and said, "Breakfast?"

"On the q.t.," said Scotty.

"Okay. That diner couple miles up the highway."

"Suits me."

"Eight?"

"Okay."

"Check."

Then Dean shuffled over to Chief John and asked him the woman's name.

"Sara Donaldson," said the chief, proudly.

"Age?"

"Twenty-four."

He was about to further this interrogation when down the stairs there suddenly clomped a long line of John's men, the township auxiliary police and members of the civil defense unit. They came wearing work shirts, dungarees, and heavy shoes—for the most part a fraternity of good-hearted, beer-bloated citizens stuck in the routine of workaday nothingness, hungry for men's-magazine-type adventure. John met them at the foot of the stairs and they talked, and agreed that the auxiliaries should immediately form a cordon around the vicinity and let no one in or out except by way of the lane from the road, and only to view the exterior of the house without trampling evidence. The auxiliaries paused long enough to utter muted sounds of horror, disgust, and determination to catch and punish the maniac responsible.

The maniac responsible—introduced in a mumble by one of the auxiliaries—became a key phrase. Even Cory had it on the tip of his tongue when he approached Dean a moment later.

"Hey," Cory growled, surprising Dean in the act of contemplating the auxiliaries contemplating the corpse. "What paper?"

"Chronicle. That's the—"

"Yeah, yeah, I know, the valley paper. What's your name?"

"Dean."

"Mine's Cory, Ed Cory."

They shook hands.

"What kind of a maniac would do a thing like this?" asked Cory, imbuing the question with declaratory intonation.

"Boy, you never know, do you," said Dean.

"Nope. What's your deadline?"

A real hound, thought Dean. "Ten for the first edition. What's yours?"

"My boy, you're lucky. Yes sir, you guys on these little papers don't know how nice you have it. I got half an hour to phone in for the first run."

"That so," said Dean.

"Yeah, what a business. Put a man in the bughouse if he ain't careful."

"Sure can."

"You know the lady?"

"Huh? Oh no, not personally. Saw her around."

"Thought you little-paper guys knew everybody."

"Yeah?"

"Yeah. Hell, I started out on a metropolitan and I been on it ever since. Started when I was a fresh kid, sixteen, copyboy. Back in the days when you brought the whisky with the pastepot."

Dean forced an agreeable grin.

"The old days," said Cory pointedly, rocking up on his toes.

"Um," said Dean.

"Nowadays, they take them fresh out of college, put them right to work. Bachelors degrees and masters degrees, why hell, we even got a Ph.D. to pencil science stuff. How about that?"

"Yeah."

"But I got my education right here, right down here on the beat, right here with my nose in it. Yes sir, Ph.D. college of hard knocks."

"Yeah."

"No diploma. No formal education."

Dean jerked his head in a short, agreeable nod.

"Wouldn't have a sheepskin if they paid me. If they was to give me one I wouldn't take it."

"The old school."

"Yup, the old school."

There was a silence then, and Dean knew Cory awaited his opinion on the all-diploma newsroom. Dean felt tempted to say that as a diploma-ed newsman himself he could sympathize with Cory's outlook, but the matter seemed wildly unimportant and he couldn't pretend enough enthusiam for a convincing lie, so he said nothing.

"You know, back in those days," continued Cory, rocking up on his toes again, "a man had to prove his worth. He didn't just strut in with a hunk of paper and get union wages, no sir. No union in them days. A man had to get out in the field and dig and come up with something."

Dean began glancing about, searching for an excuse to get away from Cory, who rambled on:

"Yes sir, we lived hard, drank hard, fought the competition with everything we had, turned out papers with guts."

"That was back in the good old days," said Dean.

"That's right," snapped Cory, suspicious of Dean's tone. "The good old days. Don't think that's just a cliché."

"Well, we still castigate the castigatable," said Dean. "Things haven't changed too much, have they?"

"Say, I'm not sure I like your attitude, son. They sure have changed, changed plenty. All you young punks do is hang on the telephone and clutch your precious diplomas."

"Pretty bad shape, eh."

"Damn right, bad shape."

"All right, all right," said Dean, "I'll take your word for it."

Cory was becoming overwrought. His toe-rocking was no longer gracefully pompous; it had become quick, nervous, a jumpy indication of anger.

Dean interrupted him as he was rocking up and taking another breath in preparation for another adamant statement. "Hey, we'd better get busy here, man. It'll be time for you to phone in pretty soon."

Cory came down on his heels with "Yeah." Then, as an afterthought, a reconciliation, said, "Just stick with me. I'll show you the ropes."

"Fine," said Dean, glad to salvage a speck of friendliness. Then he was saved from hunting for a way to avoid following Cory about by shouts from the top of the stairs. McCarthy was yelling something about a photographer, a goddamned newspaper photographer. After Dean was certain Chief John —at the other end of the cellar—had been moved by the shouts, he started up the stairs, leaving Cory behind. Chief John was right behind him when he reached the top, just in time to catch sight of the flickering beam of a camera's flash bulb bouncing from the kitchen walls. This was quickly followed by a furious howl from McCarthy. Good old Charley, Dean felt certain, had snapped his first picture— valiant auxiliary policeman guarding the door to the scene of the horror, possibly an auxiliary whose expression reflected the drama and tragedy of the scene, whose wide eyes and stunned face told graphically the shocking story of a woman with a hatchet in her skull and the discovery thereof by local, all-hallowed local police.

Valiant auxiliary McCarthy was glaring at good old Charley when Dean and Chief John got to him. McCarthy glared and growled and his posture indicated he was on the brink of violence. The chief gripped McCarthy's upper arm with gentle persuasiveness and steered his bulk out of the narrow doorway. While the chief was patiently listening to McCarthy's tirade, Charley slipped off before his entrance through the front door could be denied and went around to the cellar door. Dean left the two policemen to meet Charley from the inside of the cellar and arrived just in time to watch Charley make it through a gang of busy detectives and lab technicians at the cellar doorway by tactfully stepping around those making plaster molds of footprints in the mud. He entered the cellar, quickly took advantage of the floodlights set up by the crime lab photographer, and went to work on shots of the scene. The detectives in the cellar responded to his presence by either inclining downstage front and center in a cluster about the body, or by retreating upstage away from the body, each according to his own attitude toward the press. Scotty stationed himself downstage front and center at the focal point. Charley shot the group of conferring detectives from a low angle. He went about it silently and they silently ignored him. Charley avoided pointing his camera at the corpse until he had shot half a dozen pictures of the detectives, a couple of the coroner, and one of Chief John descending the cellar stairs. Then he joined the county crime photographer and snapped half a dozen shots of the victim. Dean sat on the third step from the bottom and watched, removing himself only to avoid being caught in Charley's shot of Chief John descending.

By now the cellar was crammed with detectives, policemen, auxiliary policemen, visiting policemen and more photographers and reporters were arriving. Funeral directors were on their way by ambulance, at least one doctor was due any minute, and there was no longer enough room in the one-room cellar for anyone to do much of anything. Even the corpse was crowded. One auxiliary, knocked off balance by the jostling, had to step into the spot of concrete between the bare legs to avoid coming down with his heavy work shoe on her shin. Dean's position on the third step was likewise overrun, so he decided to leave. He stood, caught Scotty's eye, then picked his way wearily up the stairs past McCarthy—now subdued and helpless before the flow of traffic he thought he had been assigned to prohibit—and out into the morning.

The little lane, about one city block long, was hopelessly jammed with automobiles and people now, and Dean congratulated himself for having parked his car along the road. Two television cameramen were arguing with a group of auxiliaries, and stretcher-bearing ambulance attendants were trying to make their objections to the blockade heard from well back in the packed crowd around the front entrance. Some man was shouting, "Let the doctor through," and the radio station's station wagon was beeping and inching its way up the lane behind the ambulance. Dean took a deep breath, then waded into the mob, a mixture of neighbors and strangers. He sloughed off all questions and objections to his determination to push through, and listened to the gossip as he pushed. Newcomers to the scene—people who had stopped on their way to work or had heard about the tragedy and had come running to find out about it firsthand—asked the questions. They were being told Mrs. Donaldson had been a fine woman, such a nice person, a hard worker, and what would become of the boy now, with his father and mother both dead? Oh yes, his father's dead—died of leukemia, was just getting his law practice started when he died of leukemia and left her with all those doctor bills to pay. Must have bothered her plenty, too, 'cause plenty of nights she couldn't sleep. She'd get up and read in the living room. But she never complained, just pitched in and worked, oh my how she used to work to pay those bills and keep the boy in nice clothes all the time. Such a fine young woman. Why did such a thing have to happen to her? Makes a person wonder, don't it. And the poor child, next door, crying, isn't sure what happened, poor little boy, keeps calling for his mommy. You could understand it, maybe, if she had been a different kind of woman, but she was so particular about the company she kept, such a nice person. Poor child.

He emerged from the crowd, slid and walked down the lane, now tracked and rutted, and beeped his way through the snarl's motorized tailend. He decided to take the long way back to town rather than turn around and backtrack along congested Swamp Run Road.

SPEED 35 MILES

THE WHISKY FOR MEN OF ACTION
SMOOTH AS SILK   NO BITE   NO BURN   ALL THE HARSH-
NESS FILTERED OUT

He switched on the car radio, just in time for:

Here's a bulletin just in
A beautiful
young
Ridiculee Township widow
was found murdered by a sex fiend
in the basement of her home
early this morning.
She was found
with an ax buried in her skull
with her clothing disheveled.
She was Sara Donaldson
wife of James Donaldson
a promising young attorney
who died last November
in Memorial Hospital.
Police have no doubts
that the heinous crime was the work
of a sex maniac.
They suspect that
possibly
a prowler familiar with the district
is the man who will be
the object of a statewide manhunt.
And now
for an on-the-spot news report

we switch you to Jack Walters
in the WIX roving mobile news unit
at the scene of the shocking tragedy.
Come in
Jack.
(*Static, sounds of cars in the background,
occasional sounds of people.*)
This is Jack Walters
in the WIX roving mobile news unit
at the scene of one of the most brutal
murders
ever
in the history (*Static.*)
Police say the woman
(*Static.*)
with a hatchet in her head
the blade buried in her skull
(*Static.*)
that a bloodthirsty fiend
is responsible.
(*Static.*)
and also that her clothes were torn off.
There is no doubt about it
(*Static.*)
maniac loose somewhere in this county.
Police say orders
to pick up known sex offenders
(*Static.*)
and any information you might have which
will aid in the capture and conviction of
the killer
will be appreciated.
This is Jack Walters
in the WIX roving mobile news unit
returning you now

to Herb Duncan
at WIX.
(*Sounds of static and scene noise cut by
humming quiet of radio station studio.*)
This is Herb Duncan
at WIX
and now
for the rest of the morning's news
at home and around the world
complete news reports
up to the minute.

SIP IT   TASTE IT   SAVOR ITS UNMATCHED FLAVOR

He drove on, oblivious to the latest happenings at home
and around the world, vaguely hoping this obliviousness
would purge the hodgepodge of incongruities which had inundated his mind and emotions. He was thankful when the
newscast was over and music came on, thankful until he
heard:

*I've got you
under my skin,
I've got you
deep in the heart of me*

Before breakfast with Scotty at eight, he would have time
to wash and dress and think, but not sleep. After breakfast,
he would have time to get to the bureau by nine, write the
lead story in an hour, and take the half hour after deadline
to write a sidebar. And, he told himself doggedly, Scotty
might give him the proper slant, the proper approach and
perspective for the story. After breakfast with Scotty, he
would have semi-official backing, and maybe some information.

He didn't turn on the radio in his apartment when he got
there. He peeled off his clothes and took a leisurely shower.
Then he shaved and dressed for the day. The quiet of his

small efficiency and the muffled sounds of morning activity in surrounding apartments soothed and restored him, and as he sat gazing out a window at the morning activity on the street below he began trying to force his mind to sound out possible leads for the story he would soon be typing onto copypaper.

A fiend . . .

No.

A pretty, young widow . . .

No.

Detectives today were investigating . . .

No.

Detectives were investigating today . . .

No.

An attractive widow was found with a hatchet . . .

No.

An attractive, widowed mother was attacked and . . .

No.

Through his door, from all the way across the hall he could hear her radio blurting music. He wondered how last night's session had affected her. On the pretense of bearing news of a brutality she would soon learn of by radio, he might, he speculated, lift and drop her golden V-shaped knocker and find out. No. She would hear about it and wonder if he had been at the scene, had, with the mythical dispatch of the press, brought his sleepless eyes and ears to the scene, and she would ask him, either by phone this morning or this evening when they met. He would, he decided, allow her curiosity to simmer, and then he would feed its hunger slowly, bringing himself to her as messenger, less interested in the horrible matter than she, more interested in her interest, but not obviously so; interested in her interest as sensitive to her sensitivity, to her dainty, pink-laced, feminine sensitivity. He wondered if it would be best to describe the spreadeagle nudity in detail, or to hint and encourage her mind to plunge itself senses first into the image and thus carry her closer to the matter close to him. Or was that necessary? Or beneficial? Or would it build a thicker wall? He didn't know and speculated that only a more thorough knowledge of that part of her which she denied herself would give him firmer ground for deciding, and knowledge would take more time.

More time?

He heard her door click open, then shut, and her heels tip-tap down the hallway, away.

A pretty mother was raped and massacred . . .

No. That's the one Cory will use.

He sat and smoked another cigarette to help consume ten minutes before leaving for the diner up the highway. Then he merged into the workbound traffic, into the orderly chaos, and felt a vigorous glow of purposefulness gain momentum inside himself, despite his lack of sleep.

Scotty was there when he arrived, sitting with his pointed chin resting in the palm of his hand, staring out the diner window, past the horizontal movement of cars and trucks along the four-lane highway, past the service station on the other side of the highway, staring far out into himself. Dean slid into the seat across from him. By way of acknowledging Dean's presence, Scotty scratched his wiry, graying blond hair. They ordered, then Dean said, "I see what you mean about Cory."

"What?"

"Cory. You said he's punchy. I see what you mean. He came up to me when we were in the cellar and started giving me a lot of rubbish about the good old days."

"Did he? Yeah, he's a case, all right. I wish they'd turn him out to pasture, but I guess he's there for life. You know, that job he has—it's not a job with him, it's a disease. He hangs out at headquarters all day long, all day, and then he even checks in before going home to sleep, after dinner."

"He does?"

"Yeah! Then, when he gets home—home is the Rockaway Hotel, that dive down on Wycoff Street—he sleeps with a squawkbox. He pays the bellhops to wake him up if they hear anything. Yeah! Can you beat that? He keeps one squawkbox in his room and another in the bellhops' locker room."

"What a business, the newspaper game."

Scotty sipped his coffee in agreement.

"Ah, well," said Dean, "what can you do? Anyway, what do you think?"

"About that?" Scotty waved a spoon toward the highway.

"Yeah. Got any prospects?"

"Humph. We got a thick file of prospects. We're on that milkman, but that's just between you and me." Scotty smiled. "But hell, I don't think he's even strong enough for the job. Whoever did it, I think, would have to be pretty powerful. You know, cracking skulls is not like cracking peanuts. Anyhow, for you guys, it's good copy."

"Strange," said Dean, "when I saw her—" He sighed helplessly.

"Yeah," said Scotty.

"On the concrete floor—"

"Yeah."

"I can't believe it. I've seen it but I still can't believe it."

"You won't," said Scotty, "until you understand the motive."

"The motive! So beautiful! Why would anyone want to *kill* her?"

"That's what I mean. Until you understand that, you won't believe it. When you understand, they'll have to lock you up."

Dean snickered. "I didn't get much sleep last night, Mr. Holmes. Afraid I'm a little slow today."

"Stick with it. You'll get there."

"Where? Locked up?"

"Or where Cory is. Who knows? Don't ask me. The more I see of it, the less I care. About the *who*, I mean. The more I wonder why. Motive!"

"How about the maniac angle?"

"Sure, but how do you tell a maniac? You know that Dr. Strum, the psychiatrist the county uses? Well, talk about maniacs, he's been there and back a couple of times."

"You mean, in the . . . bughouse?"

"Sure. So don't feel bad if they haul you away one of these days. Planning a trip there myself, just to rest up, you understand."

"Well," said Dean slowly, "I have a friend who says policemen are the criminal's first cousin and writers are the criminal's country cousin. So maybe we're all crazy."

"Don't argue with that guy," said Scotty.

"Nobody can argue with him. He's a poet."

"Anyway," continued Scotty, "a couple of people say they saw a mad-looking character walking up Swamp Run last night. We'll check that and I'll let you know tomorrow. Hold it down today. Hold it down all you can."

"Sure, *I* will. But what about those city guys?"

"Don't worry about them. We have them under control. They spill more than their quota, they get slim pickings from here on in."

Dean smiled.

"But," Scotty continued, "I'm afraid this is going to be a bad one. The fact that she was young and pretty, and all that. You newspaper guys . . ."

"What about her boy? I heard somebody mention she had a boy."

"He's four years old. Slept through the whole thing, I guess. Some neighbors came and got him. I'm not sure he knows what happened yet. Name's James junior."

Dean squinted and wrinkled his face into a sick expression. "My God. First his father, now his mother."

"Yeah," said Scotty, concentrating on buttering his toast. "His father was that good-looking young lawyer—you remember him, don't you?—had leukemia, sick for a long time, needed all that blood."

"Yeah," said Dean, "I did a feature on him when they were after donors."

"She moved after he got bad," Scotty continued. "Couldn't afford that big place on Route one-oh-one." He winced. "My God, some people get more than their share, don't they. Anyway, her reputation wasn't always the best, but she's worked like a dog since he died. Had to. Cost plenty, blood and specialists, and she took a beating when she sold the new home, I'm told."

"What was her maiden name?"

Scotty fanned through his notes with his left hand while forking up egg with his right. "Demsler. Yeah, Demsler. Family lives in town."

Both ate silently for a while, then Dean asked, "Was she raped?"

"Coroner says so," said Scotty. Then he pursed his lips and said, "So does that doctor, what's-his-name."

"Wonder what kind of a fiend would do a thing like this."

Scotty continued eating in silence, ignoring the invitation to pursue speculations about the maniac responsible.

Between bites, Dean asked, "You get any prints?"

"Too early to tell," said Scotty.

"Any clues at all?"

"Maybe some footprints."

"You say you figure he'd have to be pretty powerful."

"Yeah, but you never know. If the thing happened between one and three, like the coroner thinks, then this guy, whoever he is, would have to be powerful enough to break in through the cellar door without waking the neighbors—probably with his hatchet—and powerful enough to overcome a terrified woman, and powerful enough to sink a blade in her skull. That little milkman, he's a scrawny thing. But that doesn't mean he couldn't have done it. Whoever did it whacked away at her head plenty before sinking the blade, so it could have been anyone, I guess. When I say a powerful man, I mean that's who I'm inclined to look for right off. But you have to leave room for . . . for . . ."

"For the maniac responsible, whoever he might be?"

"Yeah, you have to allow for the unbelievable."

"What's that milkman's name?"

"Now please," said Scotty, "don't call him a suspect. Not yet."

"I won't. Don't worry."

"It's William Herder."

"Just for future reference," said Dean, jotting the name on his notepad.

"He says he got up to go to work and on the way out to his car he looked in her cellar window, saw her, like that."

"But—"

"Yeah, the light bulb had been smashed. It was completely dark down there when John arrived. John got an extension and hung it up. That's what was on when I got there. So there's something screwy about that milkman's story, but it might be he was just too excited, too horrified. Probably used a flashlight through the window. Maybe saw the door open and went in. He'll tell us, once he quiets down."

Dean's mind caught the image of Mrs. Donaldson's bashed skull again and he stopped eating.

"But," continued Scotty, "there's a footpath from those backyards—hers and Herder's—to the road and there were fresh prints in the mud there, so that's a horse of another color. They were made by a big man."

Strange, thought Dean, now stirred by that image again, the similarities between this egg-eating detective earning his living and the more realistic investigator of fictional fame. Both go like toonerville trolleys down the who-done-it line, one a toy trolley existing in the mind, the other a real trolley abstracting in the imagination. And now, which is which with Scotty? Does he know, after so many years of being what he has to be to earn his pay and also what he is expected to be by mystery lovers?—does he know who he really is?

"Have you," Dean asked, "ever been absolutely sure? After a thing like this is solved, I mean?"

"Don't think so," said Scotty. "Not on a case like this, where you start with this and hunt."

"Sometimes I think the whole mess is a take-off on a mystery movie. You have the good guys and the bad guys, the chase, protagonists and antagonists, hero and villain, and news media making sure the whole thing is exciting, capture climactic, trial dramatic, execution satisfying—always keeping the whole mess simple, much simpler than it really is. My friend the poet calls it society's delightful hobby—picking nasty weeds carefully. Don't disturb the roots. I guess in a way he's right. Pull at the roots and there's no telling who'd be the first to feel it."

"Aw, leave the roots of crime to the sociologists," said Scotty.

"Right," said Dean. Then he thought: but I have a hunch Beethoven knew more about the roots of crime than any sociologist.

"Well," said Dean, "I'm just a simple reporter. Just blabber about what you've found out."

"And what we haven't found out?"

"Naw, never that. Which reminds me," said Dean, picking up Scotty's check, preparing to leave, "do you want a credit line?"

"Credit line?"

"Yeah. You know, a mention. Your name."

"No," said Scotty. "I'm not running for anything."

"That's what they all say."

"No," said Scotty, picking his teeth, "no credit line. Not yet. Maybe later."

"Oh, what about her statistics?"

"Well, she was twenty-four, worked for that law firm in the building next to yours, kept to herself since the husband went. You know the rest."

"The rest?"

"As much as I know, I mean."

Dean paid the bill, listened to the neat ringing of the cash register, inspected the waitress's plump bosom as she disposed of the bill and counted out his change, then joined Scotty outside in the diner's parking lot. Scotty stood picking his teeth, staring past the highway traffic, blue eyes placid.

"I don't know how you're going to handle this story," said Scotty, "but I hope you don't go overboard."

"I'm not entirely free to handle it the way I'd like to," said Dean.

"Well," said Scotty, now lost in some silent contemplation which transported his attention, "I'll see you later."

Driving back, Dean's mind wove one part of that which would go into his story when he wrote it.

> Who?
>> One of us.
> What?
>> Has a skullful of hatchet.
> When?
>> Now.
> Where?
>> Here.
> Why?
>> Yes, why. Because why.

His mind wandered from the why and the horror to the grotesque curiosity about the horror, and he buzzed with a desire to out-grotesque that curiosity by writing:

> Whahoo, ladies and gentlemen, hang onto your seats. Gramps, tap out your pipe a minute and dust off your bifocals. Grandma, set your knittin' aside and slow that rocker to readin' speed. Pappy, disengage yourself from that pornographic girdle advertisement. Mom, untangle yourself from dishes, martyrdom, and dream world. Junior, unhand that thing. Missy, uncurl yourself from the couch. Noses up,

folks, here comes a gooder. A lady with good thighs, smooth and pink and inviting, and with spare but substantial buttocks and hips, with slim willowy waist, with firm, up-pointing breasts, with pert face, a woman in the prime of life, a woman glowing with an inviting texture, with an inviting magnetism. . . . Said beauty, to whom every red-blooded American male would thrill, given the chance, either actual or vicarious, this woman was raped. She was also killed and is no longer among us. This is a shame. But I know you do not wish to be bored by unamusing images, so I will get to the point. Some one of us—you or you or you—broke into her home last night, attacked her or lured her to the cellar and there did bash in her skull and did rape her. Or raped her and bashed in her skull. Which came first is unknown. Maybe whichever one of you performed this unfashionable feat will step forward and offer us a firsthand account. Rest assured, if you do, we will utter tisk, tisk, tisks whenever you take a breath preparatory to narrating your account, then we'll snap into complete and reverent silence when you speak, and we'll pick up our tisk, tisk, tisking where we left it when you break speaking for the taking of another preparatory breath and we'll catch our breaths again when you continue. And so it will go— our utter silence while you speak, our tisk, tisk, tisking to flood the moments of silence while you suck in another breath to continue speaking. Tisk, talk, tisk, talk. We beasts will, when you have finished, call you a beast and, because you rode the momentum of your lust to the point of no return, where, by its unchecked momentum, it carried you with it as it broke the barriers of its purpose and destroyed itself in a spasm of indulgence to become a caricature of itself. . . . Because of this we will, in all our piousness, in all our goodness, with due regard for law and order of our own design, with proper pomp and circumstance, with frontpages raving, radios blaring, T.V.'s imaging, murder you, my friend. This as you can well understand firsthand from previous experience, will give us much satisfaction.

WE'RE TURNING PRICES UPSIDE DOWN

He drove, with the image of her bashed skull, hatchet protruding, to the newspaper's town bureau office and parked by a parking meter in front of the office.

THE RIDICULEYE CHRONICLE   LINK BETWEEN TOWN AND COUNTY   WANT ADS GET THE JOB DONE   FOUR EDITIONS DAILY EXCEPT SUNDAY   LARGEST CIRCULATION

Harriet, fuzzy-sweatered, snug-skirted, hopelessly pensively hopeful of something far off, was at her desk by the door. She greeted him with the usual wistful, speculative gaze and greeting. Harold, the circulation manager, was at work on his chart of papers sold, bringing it up to date, colored-penciling it into a simple graphic expression of his company-inspired hopes and fears, his failures and accomplishments. Howard, the advertising space salesman, was likewise there, with his feet propped on his desk, wearing the bent, smug smile he used to blend himself into the mold of sanity and commerce and hide his hate for it, the smile which allowed part of him to flap freely untrampled by the heavy boot of that which he felt oppressed the rest of him.

Harriet said, "The desk has been trying to reach you."

"That's funny," said Dean. "But, anyway, tell the desk to put its extremities back on the floor, I'm here. And tell them

I'll have their bloody morsel ready for consumption in a few minutes."

"You mean the murder?"

"Deedy do."

Howard scratched his neck and smiled his gaze clockward.

Harold burst into immediate and excited chatter. "Big story, hey?"

Dean winced at Harold's wide, bonus-adding eyes.

Harold continued. "Did you hear about that woman in the township?" He addressed this to the others. "Murdered with an ax or something. Boy, and she lives right near me, too. Wow! I'll tell you something, when I heard that on the radio, I damn near crawled out of my skin." Harold had the undivided attention now of everyone but Dean, who was setting up his typewriter for the job at hand.

"Yeah, that's what the radio said. This guy, somebody, comes along last night or this morning, sometime, and butchers this poor woman, a widow, the wife of that lawyer that died last year."

Dean fought a dizzy spell as Harold continued his elated recounting of the gore. For a moment, Dean was sure he would lose his breakfast, but the pressure, the need to begin his story immediately relegated sickness to an inconsequential position, lacking priority.

His readers would, he thought as he rolled a sheet of yellow copypaper into his typewriter, already know about it when the story he would write came to them, but there would be something about the black ink on newspaper, the words, the imagery of phrases coming vaporously from the inky paper to them, silently, directly. Why read the story when it comes out in the paper after listening to it radio-jabbered all day long? He told himself it was because it isn't really accepted as reality until it says so in the paper, in black on paper. Then and only then does classified reality illuminate the illusion gloriously, really.

Harold's excited chatter continued as Dean wrote:

A young, attractive

No, not pretty or beautiful, damn it. *Attractive*

woman

Not girl or widow or mother. Not yet.

was brutally attacked and murdered

Dash? Comma? What the hell. Bow thou to the typography of it. Dash.

—apparently by a

Sex maniac? Ah, Harold, that has the impact you need for your bonus next quarter, doesn't it. And, Brady, it has what you need for the game you play, too, doesn't it. Because John Q., it has what you demand, the pure symbol of lusty horror your senses crave to caress. So be it. Who am I to fight it?

sex maniac—in her home just off Swamp Run Road, Ridiculee Township, sometime last night or early this morning.

She was Sara Donaldson, age 24, widow of the late James T. Donaldson, an attorney who died of leukemia last November shortly after passing his bar examination.

The couple had one son, James Jr., age four.

Cry, gentle ink-squinters, but not so you feel the impact of it—the four-year-old alone now, with neither father nor mother, not so you feel the impact of it deep within yourselves. Cry instead so the tears tickle down your cheeks, nicely nicely.

Local police

All-hallowed local police.

> and county detectives
> theorized her assailant was a psychotic
> who gained entrance into the Donald-
> son home by forcing open a cellar
> door.
> Mrs. Donaldson's body

Here it comes, dear reader, the set of phrases guaranteed to trip the mechanism and set your senses and instincts reeling with delighted horror.

> was discover-
> ed by a neighbor, William Herder, a
> milkman, who noticed lights on in the
> Donaldson home when he was leaving
> for work at 3 A.M. today.
> She was found with the blade of a
> hatchet embedded in her skull.
> Her housecoat had been torn open
> and her underclothes fiendishly ripped.
> She had apparently been raped.

There Pops. Now you can relight your pipe and puff. Ripped and torn. Now on we go.

> Deputy Coroner William O. Mc-
> Cracken tentatively placed the time of
> death at between 1 and 3 A.M. and
> said that in his opinion the woman
> had definitely been sexually assaulted.
> An autopsy is scheduled for late
> today.

Always an autopsy.

> A team of detectives and crime
> laboratory specialists

Oh boy. Team . . . specialists, they'll like that.

converged on the scene of the tragedy shortly before dawn. They hope to be able to come up with a lead to the identity of the murderer from clues found

I hope.

in and a-round the Donaldson home.

Known sex deviates are being rounded up for questioning and a stranger to that area of the township described as "mad-looking" is being sought.

The stranger reportedly was seen walking along Swamp Run Road near the Donaldson home last night.

Mrs. Donaldson, since the death of her husband, had been employed as secretary by the law firm of Yeats, Mancini and Hrankovich in Ridiculee.

She was described by neighbors as a "nice woman whose entire life was wrapped up in her son."

Not to mention medical bills.

She lived in a neat, newly painted cottage situated in a small community of homes near Krutcher's Corners.

Neighbors said she was an industri-ous person, pleasant and particular about the company she kept.

She commuted to and from her job by bus. She did not own a car, ap-parently because of the heavy financial burden left by her husband's lengthy illness.

Mrs. Donaldson had moved to her present home about a year ago, after

> her husband's fatal illness disabled him.
> The couple had lived in a sprawling,
> fashionable home overlooking Route
> 101.
>
> James, Jr., unable to fully compre-
> hend the tragedy of his mother's sud-
> den and violent death, was taken in
> by neighbors.
>
> He kept calling, "Mommy, Mommy,
> Mommy."

Dean rose, gathered up the copypaper, handed it to Harriet
and hurried to the washroom in the rear of the office. He
leaned over the basin and lost his breakfast. He swore to
himself as he rinsed his mouth with water, then returned to
his desk.

Harriet was at the teletype sending the first part of the lead
story. The obituary would be handled at the main office. His
story would be rewritten.

         If I had the cards to bid seven no-trump, Brady
would double—on principle, even if he didn't have it. Best
to start the bidding low.

              Ridiculee, Ridiculeye; hip hooray for the
FBI.

He leaned back in his chair, lit a cigarette, and let his arms
hang loosely toward the floor. He listened to the tense discussion going on between Harold and Howard. It whirled
around the murder, like a hurricane around its eye, and swept
along leaving a wake of chaos. It had already blown into such
crevices as the lack of adequate police protection in the
township, speculation about the late Mrs. Donaldson's financial circumstances, circumstances which had caused her to
move from her home on the hillock overlooking the highway
to the small house off Swamp Run Road; speculation about
her sex life since the illness of her husband. Howard said he
knew such and such and Harold agreed that she did have a
reputation in her younger days but that he didn't think there

was much to those other stories. Harold said he couldn't understand what would make someone commit a crime like that, so vicious and unreasonable, and Howard agreed that it was a horrible, unthinkable, unreasonable, awful thing and wondered just how safe people really were with a maniac who would do a thing like that running loose. Harold pointed out that the laws were not stiff enough, that deviates were let out of jail to roam the street, sex deviates who had records for God-only-knows and worse, and how about that. Howard said yes, that that was indeed at the root of this thing, the fact that the laws were lacking, that sex deviates were permitted to roam at large, known sex deviates, sex maniacs with police records. Harold said he knew one case where some guy was found with a ten-year-old girl and got sent to a mental hospital instead of jail, and not only that but that this guy was out now, cured they said, out roaming the streets, so you never know. No, you never know, Howard agreed, and then said he knew of a similar case, and couldn't understand why, instead of spending all that money on foreign aid they didn't spend some time and money on those laws and those deviates who do things like that and see that they're kept out of circulation. Harold agreed and said he just couldn't imagine what got into a person to make him do a thing like that, butcher an innocent woman with a four-year-old boy to take care of, a widow to boot; he just couldn't imagine what would make a man do such a thing. Howard agreed and said he couldn't either, that people like that should be done away with, prosecuted to the limit of the law, given the gas chamber, not put in institutions and then let out to roam the streets and do it again. Harold then asked Dean if it was true the woman had been raped. Dean said yes, it was true, because the coroner had . . . because her clothes had . . . because she was . . . yes it was true, or at least that's what it looks like. While Dean was wondering how the rape of a woman with a hatchet in her skull would be possible, considering how a skulled hatchet would not inspire the flow of the juices necessary for vaginal entry, Harold burst into a tirade about how it wasn't safe for a woman to be alone, especially out there in the wilds of Ridiculee Township, and how there should be some way of protecting people, some way of keeping maniacs like that behind bars, saying what kind of a township was this that would not protect its citizens any better than that, what were they all paying taxes for anyway. Howard, to bring Harold's voice down an octave, wrinkled his brow and nodded toward Harriet, who seemed to be concentrating on sending the story, but. Harold put his hand over his mouth and smiled sheepishly. Howard gave Harold a look which asked, did you forget you were in the presence of young, possibly flowered womanhood? Harold bowed his head for a moment of shame. Howard then came through with more talk about how these township police were nothing but political bums anyway and what could you expect from a bunch of political bums; that the chief had once been tried for fraud, that half the force were in on that disorderly house the county raided last fall and that the county wouldn't have raided it if the township boys had cut the county boys in on it. Harold leaned forward to catch every word and affected an expression of serious surprise, but not a surprise so serious as to be disbelieving. Howard went on to say he knew one cop in the township who dated one of the girls who worked in that same house. Harold responded properly. Howard said he'd heard they were seen together in upstate New York by one of the local merchants and that the cop had told the merchant if there was ever anything he could do for him, just give him a call.

While the Howard-Harold exchange continued, a call came through from Brady.

"Hey," said Brady, "were you out there?"

"Sure I was out there," said Dean. "I was there first, before the county detectives."

"Hmm. Good. But what's the idea about all this stuff about what the neighbors said about her?"

"I think it would be good to leave that in," said Dean. He now realized he had rationalized them into the story in order to avoid using an official source, and maybe to avoid some gore, so he rationalized some more. "We may need them before this thing is over."

"What do you mean, need them? What's the matter with your contact with the county detectives?"

"Nothing. It's just that some things the county wants to hold up on can be gotten from the neighbors, if we're careful."

"Well, all right. But this story, it's a—it'll have to be put together better than this. Why didn't you handle one thing at a time and get to the neighbors, if you had to, last?"

"Want a sidebar?" said Dean mincingly.

"A sidebar? What's the angle?"

"Oh, the house and the crowd, chronological, eyewitness, that crap."

"You say you were there first, 'eh."

"Yup."

"Okay. Bat it out and make it snappy. Stick to the sob stuff. No Hemingway, just cry. And keep it brief, as short as you can. We'll milk the pictures. And that's another thing; why didn't you call Charley as soon as you heard about it?"

"Why? Because I wasn't sure what was up until I got there, that's why. You want Charley on your neck because I got him out of bed for nothing?"

"Okay, you got answers. Finish this and give me that sidebar. And as soon as you finish that, get back there and see if you can come up with a new lead. Anything. Christ, those city papers will smash us unless we get something good and new for the second and third runs."

"Okay."

"Bear in mind that the radio and TV will ride this son of a bitch hard and we can't let them beat us. Not on this."

"Don't worry too much about them," said Dean. "The TV guys didn't even get inside the house and the radio's station wagon got stuck in the crowd. Besides, the radio and TV will only tease 'em. As proof of this, allow me to quote from the cover of Editor and Publisher." He picked the magazine out from under a pile of notes, discarded copy and old newspapers and read. "I quote, As a news medium, the newspaper creates an atmosphere of action and believability. And because advertising in newspapers is regarded as news in itself, it gets more action than in any other medium. Unquote. So there."

"All right, all right. Do you realize what time it is? Get to work on that sidebar and then check in with us when you get back to her house. Now, hurry up, damn it!"

"Okay. Okay okay."

Brady slammed down his phone and Dean chuckled at his image of Brady cursing as he did so.

Beat those tomtoms.

Faster! Harder!

He dropped another piece of copypaper into his typewriter and set to work doggedly pounding out the sidebar.

> Neighbors—dazed, shocked—were standing in front of the Donaldson residence when I arrived at 4:20 A.M.
>
> Detectives and auxiliary police had not yet arrived, but the township patrol car's spotlight shone on the front of the red and white cottage.
>
> The atmosphere was charged with tragedy.

How's that, Brady?

> Some of the people had tears in their eyes.

Again I bow to thee.

> In the cellar, the body of Mrs. Sara Donaldson lay on the cold concrete with the blade of a hatchet embedded in her skull.

Is such a body feminine or neuter, Brady?

> Her housecoat had been torn open
> and her underclothes ripped off. She
> had been raped.
>
> I cannot describe the horror we at
> the scene felt when we found her.
> Some became physically ill.
>
> Township Police Chief John Wilson
> was first on the scene.
>
> He saw to it that no one disturbed
> anything which might turn out to be
> evidence—fingerprints, footprints, mis-
> placed household articles.

Localee, localeye; of us we sing.

> Then county detectives and crime
> laboratory specialists filed into the
> tragic home and silently set to work
> searching for clues to the identity of
> the maniac responsible.
>
> Dawn rose as they went over the
> premises with a fine-toothed comb. It
> was a dawn shrouded in fog, a dawn
> Mrs. Donaldson did not see.
>
> And today, grief-stricken friends
> and neighbors, township residents,
> townspeople—everyone is asking the
> same question:
>
> Why?

Yes, why. As Scotty said—

But Scotty—

In our finite way, we ask infinity why, why,
why. But even if the answer were staring us in the face,
would we godlike, immortal conquerers of nuclear fission
be able to find it?

And when Scotty asks why, does he mean *why?*
No, he means motive, that outgrowth of *why?*

Why! Whoever asks why?

What a sad joke.

What a happy tragedy.

Tee hee.

Feed the beast. Pump it full of gore, feed it
what it needs. Pour the gore down the gullet and listen to it
gurgle and the nice sound of its belch and the smacking of its
lips deliciously. But don't for God's sake, ask why—why this
hunger, this paradox, this absurd limbo. And this monster:

He x-ed out the word *why* and typed:

Who is the maniac responsible?

Then, on another piece of copypaper, he doodled this
sketch:

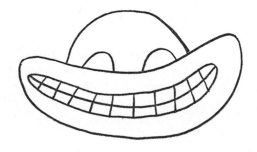

And nodded at the small sign on his desk which said:

THERE AIN'T NO REASON. IT'S THE POLICY.

Then he turned his attention to the labor of completing the
long lead story.

Howard and Harold still were engaged in their stimulating
discourse when he left the bureau office. He winked at
Harriet on his way out. She flattered him with a blush. He
reached his car just as a pistol-packing ticketeer was inspecting the parking meter. They exchanged a quick greeting,
then he drove off, unticketed.

To avoid the midmorning congestion, he turned right at the first corner and climbed a hill along a street which became a back road at the township line leading to another which led to Swamp Run Road. The uphill street was quiet, lined with shabby houses lacking the luster of recent paint, almost colorless, with porches. Here and there he saw housewives sweeping or scrubbing or washing windows.

He crossed the stream over an ancient wooden bridge, rattling loudly, and followed the narrow, twisting road into the township.

EVERYTHING FOR THE FISHERMAN   1,000 FEET

CAUTION CURVE

CARS 50
TRUCKS 40

NO PASSING

The houses here were shabbier and separated by vacant lots resplendent with the vivid green of new, unkempt vegetation. It was not suburbia; it was something left over from premobile days. The road, it seemed, was a paved deer trail. He cursed its corners, bends, dips and sudden rises over hillocks, but was glad it existed as an alternate, a way to avoid the town's congestion and Krutcher's Corners with its drive-in specializing in horror movies, its bargain barn, its comic-ghostly quality and dislocation from a more thriving past. That, he wished to avoid.

As he drove, boredom crept up and he became rocked by the dips and rises, lulled by the slow speed he had to maintain to get around the bends. He became fully aware of his lack of sleep. His eyelids sagged, his breathing slowed. His pulse beat hard and, it seemed, slowly; he lapsed into grogginess and had to provoke a fear of grogginess. He inclined his head to the left, closer to the open car window and snatched deep breaths of the dank, winter-scented spring air as it rushed past. Then he turned the window vent so it sent air directly at him.

NO MORE WORRIES FOR HIM   HE'S INSURED

STOP AHEAD

STOP

WATSON'S GROCERIES   GAS   PRICES CUT

HERE IN RIDICULEE TOWNSHIP
FOLKS READ THE CHRONICLE

He turned left onto a concrete byway and was able to travel a little faster.

SPEED 40

END 40

ART THOU READY, BROTHER?

CARS 50
TRUCKS 40

NO PASSING

The road wound into an S-curve and headed toward an old railroad trestle, abandoned now since the coal mine had shut down. Now it was an overpass to drive under.

OVERPASS AHEAD

TASTY FREEZE

Another wave of weariness hit him and he fought back.
Damn her.
And her sad tale.
And the she of her.
Had it been that first glimpse of her the day she moved in, he wondered. Her walk? The familiar something about it, as if he had seen her somewhere before, had known her before? Or had that other aspect of her brought it out? That conflict

about her, that mingling of refinement and crudeness, her act of sensuousness and innocence, of need and dead haughtiness? Who was it she reminded him of? He couldn't think who, could only repeat to himself that it had never been like this, there had never been another who spiced him so, whose form bored into his mind, exploding everything else when it did, leaving nothing but bare desire for the lovely slim roundness of her and delicious hate for the haughtiness of her put-on innocence, her method. There was something about the way she walked with such short steps and the way her spiked heels jarred her as she walked down the hardwood floor of the hallway, the loud tap, tap, tapping her heels made on the floor which jarred him and reminded him of his own heart tap, tap, tapping in its ribcage. Anticipation. A hint of something familiar, yes. But he had not seen her before. Certainly not. She was a complete stranger with a stranger's strange and sudden appeal, a stranger's silent, invisible beckoning. And he had responded to it, responded like a happy cad to an angelic juvenile nympho. He'd said . . . and she'd said . . . and he'd said . . . and she'd said not tonight because of the other guy . . . but . . . oh, all right, after he leaves. But with eyelids fluttering nervously. Excited by his excitement? Maybe. Innocence? In a way, but innocence superimposed over something else. Innocent eyes. Blue and alive; sometimes somber and introverted; sometimes bold and inviting, daring him with a challenge reluctantly thrown out to him. That might be it—her reluctance. But was she? Tonight—he would find out tonight. But how many tonights might there be! Last night?

Ah, yes. Last night she had told him, between bouts, that she had found herself with no home when her father died, that she hated living alone but didn't like living with her girlfriend either. She had told him her father died a year ago and that her mother had died before that. She had been eighteen when her father died. He had tried to steer the talk to something gay, but her father had died a year ago, she had repeated after the next bout, had died of a heart ailment. Then another bout, fraught with Eue-golly-gee-Dean this is only our first date, etcetera, and then out of a clear blue-eyed sky she had told him she was still helping to pay for the expense of her father's dying. Why couldn't he understand her position—a young girl, living alone, in an apartment of her own? Oh, he did, he did, he had told her. He understood. He had comforted her—the prelude to another bout—but she had talked of her father again. He was so good, such a good family man. Then another bout. Then the gong to end the round—her dead father. And another drink. Yes. How much had he drunk? And how much had she drunk? Stupefying, but neither had wanted to end it, to stop the useless cycle and separate for the night, she in her bed, he in his, daddy in his grave. So he had come right out and mentioned it and she had ignored his mention of it and returned to the difficulties of a young girl living alone; the buyer where she worked, the department head, everybody, and she just a poor, defenseless girl living alone. She had told it all like a knight recounting his adventures in a strange and alien land. And she, as she had told it, had emerged from the struggle against overwhelming odds heroically, unscathed, undefeated. He had left her, drunk, exhausted, aching, defeated, at 3 A.M. and had tumbled into his bed, alone, too tired to care.

But when he awoke an hour later he cared again, cared immensely, cared acutely. And yet, his desire remained that happy blend of disdain and desire. She was not the one for him, not the lifetime mate he wished he would seek, felt he should seek. She was a work of art he must experience. She was an accident of clear skin, large blue eyes, yellow hair, supple limbs and torso—a modern museum piece of eye-catching conformation. Not an imitation, and yet how long could she, if he had his way, remain such before he discovered in her beauty the desire-cooling feature which would combine with what she herself was and he was not? A combination to release him. The inevitable.

He dropped thoughts of her as he rounded a bend and came upon the clump of homes, the scene. He jammed on the brake when he spied the footpath Scotty had mentioned. He brought the car to a quick stop off the blacktop, got out, looked about, then started trudging up the path toward the house. Through the trees he could see its red and white finish. It gleamed in the sun now and the crowd in front had thinned to driblets of little groups.

This is how the killer could have done it, he thought. This is the logical thing—the path to his lust's back door. He walked like this, carrying the hatchet, maybe in his belt, feeling his way, touching these young saplings, stepping over this rock, peering around this bend in the path at the back of her house and the clearing, her backyard. Between the edge of the foliage-hidden patch of woods and her cellar door, her backyard—a clearing. But there were no lights here. The light was in the front. Her light, from her living room. Yes, the neighbors said she sometimes got up and read, unable to sleep. Only her. He must have been athrob with a vicious lust for her, desire out of control, feeding on itself. He must have skirted the edge of her backyard to her cellar door, walked down these stone steps like this, used his hatchet to pry open the door, entered, paused, like this, for a moment, listening, like this, then—

Then tiptoed over to the foot of the stairs, called her name or made a noise. Sara? Oh, Sara? Maybe she heard him calling. Or maybe it was a noise, the sound of him breaking in. That was likely. And then she came to the top of the cellar stairs, opened the door, asked, Who's there? Yoohoo, who's there? Frightened. Then switched on the light in the cellar from the switch in the kitchen. Frightened. And he must have ducked under the stairs, like this, right here. There was the light on, right there, over the spot where he left her, and here he was, right here, under the stairs, and then she came down. He waited. She hesitated, then continued. He could feel the hatchet, heavy and balanced, pressing the heel of his palm as it hung by his side in his loose fingers. Then she saw the opened cellar door and thought the mystery of the noise had been cleared up. The door. She must have forgotten to lock it, she thought. She came down the steps quickly now and crossed to close the cellar door. And in two quick movements he lunged from here and smashed her skull with the hammer of the hatchet. She fell to the floor in a crumple of housecoat and long tresses of hair. Maybe she was only stunned and tried to get up and he used the hatchet again, smashed her again, then again, then again. She must have crawled a little, toward her right, and ended here, with the blade being sunk into her brain, pulled out, sunk again, pulled out, sunk and left there. And the light bulb—he smashed that, maybe with the flat of the hatchet blade. Then—

"Hello!" It came to him like a clap of thunder from the top of the stairs; it cut through him and left him shaky. "Where the devil did you come from?" It was Scotty, descending, wearing his usual frown over a grim smile.

"I, 'eh, came up . . . the 'eh . . . path and in through the cellar door."

"Well, don't look so guilty, Dean. That path's been gone over with a fine-toothed comb. Don't worry, we won't end up with your footprints."

"That's gratifying," blurted Dean, trying to sound casual, still trembling. "I was chased out here by Brady. Wants a new angle for the later editions."

"Well, about all I can tell you is they're combing the woods around here, hunting for anything, a clue. So far, nothing."

"Fine-toothed comb. The township police?"

"The whole lot of them."

"Well, I'll phone that in," said Dean, "and get out of your hair."

"Hey," said Scotty, "how did you manage to slip up that footpath without being stopped?"

"Who was supposed to stop me?"

"Oh, one of John's auxiliary policemen, but I guess he got

bored and left to go hunting in the woods with the others."

"Where was he posted?"

"On the path, near the road."

"I didn't see a soul."

"Sure? Maybe they all left. Supposed to be a few stay behind, around here."

"I've been thinking," said Dean. "Do you think the killer used that path?"

"Could have," said Scotty. "Could have done a lot of things. Might have been in here to begin with. I'm inclined to think, the longer I'm here, that she must have known him and let him in."

"Yeah," said Dean, pleased by this version, "or there would have been some signs of a struggle."

"Not necessarily, but it's a possibility."

"Well," said Dean haltingly, "guess I'll go make my phone call."

"Help yourself," said Scotty. "The other hounds of your breed have come and gone. Only you have returned to the scene of the crime. The phone's all yours."

Dean lumbered up the stairs, again feeling the effects of sleeplessness—this time in a spell of dizziness—to the kitchen and living room and phone. When his call had gone through to the desk, he told Brady his new lead. Brady grumbled and switched him to Ken. Dean dictated:

"A battalion of police combed the wooded area around the Donaldson home in Ridiculee Township late this morning seeking clues to the identity of the sex maniac who murdered Mrs. Sara Donaldson.

"Then fill in from the other, then—

"All fulltime township police were assigned to the investigation. They are being aided by auxiliary, civil defense units, firemen, town police, and county crime specialists.

"By eleven A.M. today they had fanned out to a wide radius around the community of a dozen homes where the murdered widow lived with her four-year-old son, James Junior.

"That ought to do it. We should top the city papers with this little detail about the search. Mention that to Brady, will you?"

"Sure," said Ken. "But don't they have any clues yet?"

"No, there's not a damn thing. Not yet."

"Okay, stay with it, boy. And shoot it to us if they come up with anything."

"So what else do I have to do all day?"

"Okay. See ya."

But Dean did not stay. For a month he had been wanting to drive up to the mountain on the new section of road which would, when finished, be a direct route out of the valley, away from the town to the country beyond. He called a goodbye down to Scotty in the cellar and walked down the cinder-and-mud driveway to the road to his car. He used the driveway to turn around and headed toward the mountain.

As he drove along the township's byways, the signs of human cuts into the earth and structures over it gradually receded and the two-lane road flattened out along a plain at the base of the mountain. Then he spotted the end of the two-lane concrete strip and the beginning of the new four-lane highway, divided by what would become a lane of grass. It was a scraped bare strip of earth now and both sides of the highway were flanked by shoulders of freshly scraped earth.

IMPROVED HIGHWAY AHEAD

ROAD CLOSED

UNDER CONSTRUCTION

The road-closed sign was nailed to a carpenter's horse which practically blocked entrance to the new highway, but he saw the tracks other vehicles had made around the sign onto the new road and followed them.

The road climbed straight and wide toward the mountain's round top. It went up, then leveled, then up again, in a determined succession of ascending plateaus. As he drove up the steepest rise, all he could see for a moment was the road's new, black surface banking upward, the sky beyond its crest, and the forest on either side. A moment later, he went over the top. The forest ended abruptly and to either side of the high-way, spreading gloriously to right and left, was a vista of lush, green growth, a carpet of new spring greenery sloping down and out and away to distant clumps of woods. It took his breath away. He stopped the car and gazed. It looked as if the land now under the thick carpet of new growth had once been farmed. The forest ended too arbitrarily not to have been ended by human sweat, and the distant line of the forest's continuation was decisive. But now the land was claimed by wild grasses, wild flowers, clumps of pinelike bushes, all growing in a thick tumble, helter-skelter, glowing various greens under the bright sun, completely uninhabited, untouched. If there had once been a farm here, there was but one sign of it: the abruptly ended forest. No old barn, no old farmhouse, nothing but the wild growth, running away rampant with spring.

He stepped down on the accelerator and continued up the new highway a few more miles, past where the forest resumed, wondering why he saw no equipment and men working, until he came to a bridge, shining of new steel and fresh paint. He parked by the roadside just before the road crossed the bridge and walked down the slope toward the gurgling sound of a sun-glistening mountain stream. The slope went down gradually and was littered with the signs of early spring flood—dead tree trunks, tangles of mud-caked brush, flattened grass. But now it was dry under foot and he walked with loping, resolute strides. On the other side of a row of trees, he found the stream. It was wider than he had imagined it would be this far up the mountain, and it was shallow and rapid. The moving water sparkled and sang a single, high-pitched tune to its own singularity of movement and direction. He sat down on a flat rock to listen and, possibly, sleep.

The sun was warm, so he took off his shirt and stretched his arms out, elbows resting on his knees. The sun's warmth seemed to bore into him, returning something that had been lost during the winter.

He was feeling warm and comfortable, far away from the town and the township and the murder, and was approaching sleep, listening to the stream's toneless tune and the birds and buzzing of insects when he heard a voice behind him.

"Hello, Kiddo. Nice here, isn't it."

The voice had a clear baritone ring that cut through the other sounds. He was surprised to find, when he looked back over his shoulder, an old man standing with his hands on his hips, smiling a wide-eyed, idiotic, toothless smile. He was sure the man was old because of his gnomelike shape and wrinkled skin and toothlessness, but the man also had a youthful quality: his skin seemed to have a close-pored, glowing vitality. The longer Dean looked, the younger the old man seemed, and when he spoke again, his clear baritone also seemed to belie his age.

"Seen you drive up, Kiddo. Good thing you stopped where you did. Road ends just up the way a piece. Liable to drive right off'n the road and not be able to drive back on. Didn't you see the sign?"

"Yeah, I saw the sign."

"Then what made you drive up my mountain, Kiddo?"

"I just wanted to, that's all."

"Just thought you oughta, 'eh, Kiddo?"

"That's right. I just felt like it. Who are you?"

"Live here, Kiddo."

"Whereabouts?"

"Oh, on up the mountain further, back in the woods."

"How can you live way up here? There's nothing up here."

"Ha! Kiddo, there's everything up here. On the weekend, the fishermen come up and in the fall the hunters. Rest of the time, I don't see them and that's all right, too."

"How long have you lived up here?"

"All my life, Kiddo." The old man now walked with a stiff, leaning-forward shuffle to the flat rock and sat down beside Dean. He wore an old gray work shirt, old-fashioned overalls with suspenders, and high-top shoes with soles worn thin. "Mind if I join you?" he asked, after he had seated himself.

"Not at all."

"How do you like my stream?"

"*Your* stream?"

"Sure, my stream. Whose did you think it was, Kiddo?"

"I thought it belonged to the state."

"Naw. Oh, they got titles and all that stuff, Kiddo, but don't let that fool you. This is my stream and my mountain and my woods."

"I see," said Dean a little caustically.

"No you don't," said the old man, "but that's all right. Can't blame you a bit for not seeing."

"Thank you."

The old man ignored Dean's tone and, with a quick jerk of his short arm, pointed out into the stream. "There! See that trout?"

Dean's eyes followed the line of the old man's pointing finger. It was a large trout and was holding itself in one spot against the current, waiting for food, apparently.

"That ain't my trout," said the old man cheerfully. "That belongs to the government."

"Oh," said Dean. "I understand now. You own the stream and the mountain, but you don't own the trout."

"Course I don't, Kiddo," said the old man. "State puts them in there. State stocks this stream with trout every spring. Sometimes twice, some springs. Then the fishermen come along on weekends and pull them out. Ain't my trout. He's one of them which is put in by the state and pulled out by the fishermen."

"By the way you say it, I take it you don't approve of the state's trout-stocking program."

"Oh, I don't mind it, Kiddo. Makes no difference one way or t'other. They put 'em in, pull 'em out. Mine stay."

"Yours?" Dean looked for the trout again, but it had gone.

"Yeah, mine. On up the run a ways, that's where you'll find mine. They ain't put in by the state and they ain't pulled out, neither. Them's mine, Kiddo."

"Oh."

"You needn't be so uppity, Kiddo."

"Pardon me," said Dean snidely. "I didn't realize I was in the presence of the owner of such a vast domain."

"Yeah, it's vast, all right," sighed the old man. "Can't hardly keep track of it all."

"How many in your household?"

"Just me, Kiddo."

"Just you! How do you manage?"

"I don't *manage*, Kiddo. I just live here."

"Oh, I see."

"Naw, but that's all right."

"Don't you object to them running a road right up the side of your mountain and digging a tunnel right through the top of it?"

The old man leaned his head back and laughed. "Haw! Shucks no, Kiddo. That road don't do me no harm. Course, it don't do them much good, neither, but that's all right."

"Does a lot of good," said Dean. "That road will cut off fifty miles of winding around the mountain. This way, we can drive right up, through the tunnel and down the other side."

"Few decades, maybe. Pretty soon this road will get bad, just like t'other one did. Listen, Kiddo, I've seen these roads come and go. They don't mean nothing. That's why they don't bother me, Kiddo."

"But," said Dean, becoming agitated with the old man's nonsense, "if this is your mountain, doesn't it bother you to see these roads come and go? Doesn't it bother you to see them come along and cut a wide right-of-way up the side of your mountain? And how about that tunnel? Suppose it caves in. Won't that bother you?"

"Course not, Kiddo, course not. Don't mean a thing, not a blooming thing. One way or t'other, me and this old mountain will stay."

"Oh, yeah? Well, suppose they come up with dynamite and start blasting away at this whole mountain. Suppose they drop a hydrogen bomb and remove this whole mountain. Would that bother you?"

"Course not, Kiddo. They'd have to put all this earth and rock somewheres, wouldn't they? If they blasted like you say, what would they do with all my mountain, in little pieces like it'd be? Anyway, there's other mountains. I'd just move on. Wouldn't mean a thing, Kiddo."

"Why in the hell," exploded Dean, "do you keep calling me 'Kiddo'?"

"No offense, Kiddo, no offense. You needn't get all groused up like that. Just a manner of speaking, Kiddo, that's all. Don't mean nothing by it, or if I do, I can't rightly say what it be."

"Well, I don't like the implications," said Dean. Then he stood, picked up his shirt and started walking back up the hill to his car.

"Hey, Kiddo, where you going?" The old man sounded hurt.

"Some place where you're not," said Dean. "I came up here to catch a little rest and I don't want to be bothered by an old goat with illusions of mountain-owning."

"Well, shucks, Kiddo, I didn't mean nothing."

Dean kept trudging up the hill. He didn't look back until he was inside his car. Then as he was starting the engine, he glanced down and saw the old man standing on the rock watching him.

He cut the wheels into a U turn, crossed the medial strip of earth to the lanes heading down the mountain, and accelerated with a sigh of relief. Something about the old man—he wasn't sure what—had addled him. He told himself it wasn't the old man's silly illusion of owning the mountain and the stream. That was only amusing, he told himself. And it wasn't the old man's hazy answers to questions, either. He should never have bothered to ask the stupid old goat such questions. He should have realized immediately he could not carry on a coherent conversation with him. He was obviously just an old bum, a hermit, who lived alone up here on the mountain, nothing more. He would forget the old man and find a spot where he could just lie back in the grass and feel the warm sun baking into his hide, and maybe sleep for a few minutes. After all, the old fellow was obviously demented and he hadn't driven all the way up the mountain just to listen to an old hermit's crazy chatter about the mountain being his.

Dean drove on, switching his thoughts now to marvel at how straight and smooth the new highway was, until he spotted the vista which had attracted his attention on the way up. He stopped, got out, and crossed the highway. For a moment, he stood looking back up at the stretch of road he had just driven. This must be five miles from the bridge, he thought. At least five miles, a straight five miles away from that old fool. Then he walked off the highway's new surface, over the dried earth of the road's shoulder, into the tall growth of the meadow. He drifted down through the tall grass until he was a good distance from the road, then sat down on a spot where the grass wasn't so tall. He could see the town in the distance, the tiny dots of roofs, lines of streets, far off. But he wished the old man hadn't spoiled his loneliness by the stream. He thought about how clear the water was and how the trout's shadow looked on the bottom, rippling over the smooth stones. He ran his fingers over the coarse grass and weeds and told himself that the grass, like the old man, was an alien species, but harmless. Some creature could be lurking down in the grass next to the earth, possibly something alive and dangerous, with the natural means to harm him. But it would scamper away from him, possibly driven by an innate knowledge that the upright creature is to be feared above all others. Unless it was wounded. Even then it could do him little harm, nothing he couldn't take care of by driving to a hospital in time. But if he fell and broke a leg, that would be different. That would be his own doing and it would be more difficult to get to the hospital with a broken leg than it would with a rattlesnake bite.

He found the floor of the meadow a tangle of decay through which the thick crop of new grass had managed to find a way up. It was abuzz with activity, more tangle and activity, proportionately, than the town he had left, he thought. And he was not so comfortable as he thought he would be. The meadow sloped down to woods, and they sloped down to the river. Across the river, he could see the town—that was the trouble with it, he told himself. He had come up here to get away from the town and to sleep, and now he sat watching it and it reminded him that it had been two years since he had graduated from the university and started work for the *Chronicle*. He hadn't meant to stay. He wanted to work for the *Chronicle* long enough to learn enough to move up to a bigger newspaper. He had come to the game with the usual thirst for the sights, smells, and feel of life firsthand, and a desire to play a small part in the recapture, if possible, of Jeffersonian ideals. He had believed in the freedom of the press passionately and when he found it unpracticed, unpracticeable, his zest had withered. Then he discovered the essential similarity between so-called cheap journalese and so-called slick journalese, and found only one other alternative—snob journalese. This led to a final discovery —that words are symbols, like numbers. And the longer he stayed with the *Chronicle*, the less he wanted; the more he wanted to do nothing, move nowhere, because he could see no reason to, no end to it, no worthwhile, reachable goal.

Marriage? Maybe that would change things. But who was there to marry? Certainly not one of the fearfully flippant, gum-chewing dolls behind screens of perfume he had met at the dances in town. One of them had been a fine piece, but not—no, never—a mate. Nor that wealthy one from the Heights—Sandra—well-fed, big-boned lovely, and in a taught or bottled way emancipated, roundly educated but with the instincts of a data-clogged computer. No, nor dear Sweet Reet, with her instincts of the mythical native virgin on the brink of, but inhibited by prospects of becoming an honorably, whorefully exploitive wife.

A breakdown in communications, as they say. That at least. Somewhere along the line he had lost his reverence for their beliefs, their morals, their immorality, their ideas of success. Suck-zess. At some point between leaving home for the university and now, the last shred of enchantment with all that had fallen from him, and it had left him orphaned from his own childhood. Well, he told himself, that was nothing unusual. It had happened to others before, was happening constantly. Yet somehow most of the others seemed to retain enough to get some fun out of competing in the wage-earning, workaday world. They married, had families, sat in clubs and churches. It's a thing to do, the only seemly thing to do. The unseemly capitalized on their unseemliness, which amounts to the same thing as conforming to the seemly. They all got, are getting along without worrying about why they are. True, I don't earn much, don't stand any real chance of ever earning much; but on the other hand, I don't require much—just food, shelter, and an interesting sex life. So I guess I could live reasonably, if I could only find a reason to. I should resolve right now to fit in, play a little company politics—that parody on sex—and become a mortgage-holding suck-zess. But—

> Where would it get you?
> I don't know.
> Why should you?
> I don't know.
> When should you begin?

I don't know.

When should you end?

I don't know.

Should you, not knowing where or when or why?

I don't know.

Your lack of knowing is overwhelming.

Yes, that I know.

Do others know?

Some know they don't, others don't seem to wonder about it. They know so much about the trivial things they never have to wonder about the why and where to. Their heads are full; there's no room for questions. Besides, their churches answer their big questions, or even if they don't, they pretend to and the others pretend the questions have been answered.

Pretty nifty.

For them.

But even those who wonder, don't they go in the same direction—with the current?

Yes, they seem to.

And you, despite your obstinacy, don't you go with them?

I am pulled with them, yes. I don't *go* with them

Why can't you just let yourself go?

What was that trout waiting for?

How can you avoid it?

Suicide. Which, when you get right down to cases, may be in the same general direction. The big boom—

And the stream—

Go together, nicely nicely.

So what difference does it make?

None, I suppose. None that I can see.

You see very poorly.

But I do, occasionally, see.

Then, from behind him, slicing through the rustle and whistle of a rising wind, cut the sound of the old man's voice.

"Hello, Kiddo."

It drove into his thoughts, disrupting him, but he sighed and turned and watched the old man pick his way stiff-legged down the grassy hillside.

"Where did you come from? How did you get here so quick?"

The old man cackled in a high, screeching falsetto. "Walked, Kiddo. How else?"

"You couldn't have. It's at least five miles from where I saw you last. You couldn't run five miles that fast, old man. That was just a few minutes ago."

"I know all the shortcuts, Kiddo." The old man cackled again, then plopped down in the grass beside Dean.

The old fool, thought Dean. Why is he dogging me?

"Good God, old man. Are you for real?"

"So real you wouldn't even believe it, Kiddo. How do you like the view from up here?"

"It scares me. The air's so thin."

"Well, stick around. You'll get used to that, Kiddo. Stick around for a few days and keep me company."

"I can't, you old goat, whoever you are, you great land-owner. I have to get back."

"Why, Kiddo?"

"Well, for one thing, I have a job. And, though it's certainly none of your business, I have a date for tonight."

"What job and what date, Kiddo?"

"I'm a reporter and I'm covering a murder story at the moment. I have a date for dinner with my neighbor, the girl next door."

The old man shook and squeaked with a convulsion of laughter. "Shucks, Kiddo," he finally said, breathless, "that ain't nothing. From up here you can cover plenty of murders and you can find plenty of girls next door, too."

"Old man, you're more than a little nuts. Your mind is gone."

"Yup, far, far away, Kiddo. It's the thin air. But I'm serious just the same. From up here you can smell the murder and see the mist rise every day."

"Yeah sure, but you don't get the idea, old man. I work for the paper and have to write the story."

"What story, Kiddo?"

"About the murder."

"What murder, Kiddo?"

"Young widow found with a hatchet in her skull."

"Oh, those murders."

"No, *that* murder. It's a very unusual case."

"Naw, Kiddo. Whoever told you that?"

"Nobody had to tell me. It is, that's all."

"What's so unusual about it, Kiddo?"

"It was a pretty, young widow, found with a hatchet in her skull—*in* her skull."

"Shucks, Kiddo, most everybody's got a hatchet in his skull. What's so unusual about that?"

"Look, you crazy old goat, why don't you just keep on walking till you come to an asylum."

"See, Kiddo? Even you got a hatchet in your skull. See what I mean?"

"No, I don't see what you mean, old man. But I came up here to rest, not talk nonsense with a crazy old buzzard. So how about you just toddling on down the road, back to wherever it is you come from."

The old man shook with mirth again, emitting retching, wheezing squeaks. "Kiddo, you slay me. That is, you would if you could. Damn shame. About that hatchet, I mean. Being stuck in your head the way it is."

"Yeah, damn shame."

"Want me to pull it out for you?"

"I want you to get the hell away from me, old man. That's all I want."

"Yeah, I suppose. Once a feller gets used to it being stuck in there, a feller kinda just gets used to it, huh, Kiddo. I oncet knowed a lonely old widow, picked up crabs. She come a-running up my place fit to be tied when she first found out she had them little fellers with her. Well sir, I told her it didn't make no difference anyhow, and I told her I couldn't do nothing anyway, so I told her she'd just have to send down to the drugstore at Krutcher's Corners. But you know, before she got the medicine, she got so used to having them little fellers around, she just decided to keep them. They was terrible pesky, but they was company just the same. Guess that's the way it is with your hatchet, Kiddo. You don't like it none, but you'd hate to part with it. Wouldn't you, hey?"

Dean shook his head and snorted with exasperation. "How long have you lived up here by yourself, old man?"

"I told you before, all my life, all my natural life. And then some, I guess." The old man flashed his gummy smile against Dean's frowning wrinkling together of contempt and perplexity. "You oughta stay awhile, Kiddo," said the old man, "instead of messing around with that foolishness. I'd teach you a thing or two, yes-sirree."

"About old widows with crabs?"

"Yup, them and others."

"Can't stay, old man," said Dean. "I've got to get back to town. The paper should be out when I get there, too, come to think of it. So—" He rolled and rose to his feet and turned to the old man. "—I'll say goodbye to you, you old goat."

"Well, so long, Kiddo, but remember."

Dean leaned forward and climbed slowly back toward the highway. I'll go home, he thought. Catch a nap, eat a sandwich, go back to the office later this afternoon.

"Remember the hatchet in your skull," the old man called, raising his voice as Dean's steps carried him away. "Remember I offered to pull it out."

Then, as Dean reached the top, the old man cackled again, a mad, unreal cackle which rang loudly in Dean's ears despite the wind. Dean shook his head and frowned. Then smiled to himself. "Crazy old goat," he muttered. He turned and looked back down the hillside once more. The old man, standing bent forward, was still watching him, smiling his toothless smile. The old man lifted his arm and waved goodbye, still grinning. Dean waved back.

When he returned to the bureau office, the others were preparing to leave for the day. Dean slumped into his chair and, for a time, stared out at the street where a hawker, stationed in front of the office by Harold, was doing a booming business. Harold was humming to himself as he straightened his desk top. Harriet was applying her lipstick. Howard was adding ad lineage sold that day on his adding machine.

The four editions of the day's newspaper were stacked neatly on Dean's desk. In huge type, across the top of the front page, the latest edition said:

WOMAN FOUND MURDERED

And under that, in smaller type:

POLICE SEARCH FOR
MANIAC RESPONSIBLE

Dean's sidebar, he found, started where the lead story's two-column lead ended. It ran down one column beside the body of the lead story under:

TRAGEDY DAZES,
SHOCKS THOSE
AT THE SCENE

72

Two three-column pictures were side by side under the banner and a deep two-column shot of McCarthy ran down the page under one three-column shot and beside the lead story's two-column lead. McCarthy had added the proper touch. He stared out from the ink and paper wide-eyed, open-mouthed, anguished. He looked like a monk who had just been given a medical explanation of reincarnation by Saint Peter.

The other photos showed a group of detectives gathered around Scotty, peering down solemnly at the body of Mrs. Donaldson, which didn't appear in the photo. The other three-column shot showed the Donaldson home and part of the crowd gathered in front of it, including the radio station's mobile news unit in the background, bogged down in a puddle of people.

Over a short in eight-point boldface in the lower left corner, an italic headline said:

BOOM PREDICTED

Elsewhere, and among other things, the newspaper jibber-jabbered thusly:

ONLY UNION MEN
CAN SERVE BREW

GROUP STYLE MEDICAL PLANS GROWING;
RECORD SHOWS TENDENCY TO BELITTLE

U.S. EXCEEDS SOVIET
IN MISSILE PROGRESS

GOOD MOTIVATION NEEDED
TO ABSORB EXTRA ENERGY

WAR SCARE MORE
SMOKE THAN FIRE

LIONS SEEK BLOOD DONORS

INDUSTRY ROLLING
AGAIN BUT MANY
REMAIN OFF WORK

ENJOY A WEEK IN MIAMI

SOME AGAINST DEATH SENTENCE FOR BOY, 14

SHOULD DOCTORS BE SUED FOR MALPRACTICE?

SCIENTIST'S MATE
IS SEEKING DIVORCE

KIDS SHOULD PLAY WITH OWN SEX

VICIOUS BURGLAR
KILLED BY VICTIM

ENROLLMENT
CLIMBING UP
SCHOOLS HERE

DEMOS HEAR TALK
ABOUT HYPNOSIS

PRESIDENT LEAVES GOLF
FOR DAY IN WHITE HOUSE

DESTRUCTIVENESS OF HYDROGEN BOMB
MIGHT MAKE OLD WEAPONS OBSOLETE

CAREFUL USE OF
POISON IS URGED

MAN SHOOTS GIRL
IN LOVERS LANE

"JAZZ MASS"
PACKS CHURCH

EMPLOYEES TOLD
TO END STRIKE

WELCOME TO MUDVILLE, USA,
SAYS SIGNS HELD BY WOMEN

And, in small print:

> Doctors are particularly worried about Khrushchev's high blood pressure and excessive weight and have recommended that he go more often on holiday and play golf like President Eisenhower.

And:

> DEAR MARTHA RIGHT: My boyfriend insisted that if I love him I should prove it. I do love him and so I proved it. When we first met, he told me he liked me very much and paid a lot of attention to me and flattered me and all. But later, I noticed a change in him.
>
> He just crabbed at me and told me my clothes weren't right.
>
> But I love him and want to marry him anyway, so I went right on going with him.
>
> Then he went to another town one night and stood me up and the next thing I knew, he was marrying this other girl from that town.
>
> Can you help me?
>
> Distressed.
>
> DEAR DISTRESSED: A boy that demands you prove your love doesn't love you at all. He doesn't love you and if you yield, he won't think you're very nice.
>
> That's probably why your boyfriend married the other girl—because you yielded.

But that's all over and done with now, so you've learned your lesson.

Now it's time to stop thinking in terms of "human love" and try thinking in terms of "divine love."

It's much better.

But in boldface type at the bottom of page one it kept saying:

BOOM PREDICTED

So Dean turned to the advertisements and they advised him thusly:

BUY NOW   WE'RE TURNING PRICES UPSIDE DOWN

PEACE   COSTS   MONEY   HELP   STRENGTHEN AMERICA'S PEACE POWER   BUY U.S. SAVINGS BONDS

WOMEN   SHOW   PREFERENCE   FOR   BLACK   AND WHITE COSTUMES   IT'S ONLY NATURAL

REMEMBER   A GOOD USED CAR SOLVES ALL YOUR TRANSPORTATION PROBLEMS

BREASTS   LEGS   THIGHS   OTHER TURKEY PARTS   WITH EACH $10 ORDER

ALL CARS MUST GO   TOMORROW

A   BIG   HELLO   NO   PUSSYFOOTING   DON'T MISS THIS SPECTACULAR SALE OF RUGS   UPHOLSTERY FURNITURE REDUCED

YIPPEE!   WE NOW HAVE GIRLS' TIGHTS

FOR   BETTER   BARGAINS   GO   HALLERS   IT'S IMPORTED   KNOWN BY THE COMPANY IT KEEPS

TIRE TRIUMPH   SALE   HURRY

SEE THE HOUSE ON HAUNTED HILL   TERROR RIDES AGAIN   ALSO SCREAMING SKULL   COMING SOON

NOW SHOWING   MOST OVERWHELMING
CAVALRY CHARGE EVER SCREENED   THOUSANDS OF COSSACKS
TARTARS   DEATH-DEFYING BASCHIRI
FRIGHTMARE OF MOVIE MONSTERS   UNSPEAKABLE
HORROR   SEE SLAVE MAIDENS AT THE MERCY OF HIDEOUS
BEASTS   DON'T DARE COME ALONE
LAST WEEK ONLY   RALLY ROUND THE FLAG, BOYS

LIVE BETTER BY FAR
IN A BRAND NEW CAR

IT'S SUCH A COMFORT TO TAKE THE BUS
AND LEAVE THE DRIVING TO US

IF WE DON'T HAVE WHAT YOU'RE LOOKING FOR   WE'LL
ORDER IT

ARE FACE CREAMS OVERRATED?

MEN OF DISTINCTION ARE BOURBONITES

PERMA LIFT GIRDLES AND BRAS FIT EVERY FIGURE TO
PERFECTION

GOOD NIGHT
SLEEP TIGHT
NATO STANDS WATCH

SUCH BIG VALUES!   SUCH LOW PRICES!

BEWARE! WATCH OUT FOR THIS PEST

WOULD YOU LIKE A BARBECUED HAM FREE?

COME AS YOU ARE
EAT IN YOUR CAR

NOW'S THE TIME TO REDECORATE YOUR HOME

LEARN TO LEAD WITH OUR INFALLIBLE METHOD
HEAR MEN TELL HOW THEY OVERCAME FEAR
ELIMINATED INFERIORITY COMPLEXES   MADE FRIENDS
GAINED PROMOTIONS   INCREASED INCOME   DEVELOPED
COURAGE

IT'S WHAT'S UP FRONT THAT COUNTS

ELECT SOLOMON JUDGE

PATSY DOMINICI FOR COUNCIL   AGAINST TAXES   WAGE AND SALES TAX WILL GO   WHEN PATSY COMES

WHAT WILL HAPPEN WHEN UNEMPLOYMENT COMPENSATION RUNS OUT?

IT'S TIME TO ASK YOURSELF
HOW'S YOUR MENTAL HEALTH?

A Square in Catland

The golden V-shaped knocker met him eye high. Rock 'n' roll boomed from the other side of her door. He felt the floorboards vibrating through the soles of his shoes, confirming Sweet Reet, the lowbrow hifi buff. Fine, he told himself. Toujour L'Amour, tonight for sure. Tonight, Sweet Reet, thou shalt be reamed with reality.

Prior to knocking, a short moment of rapid contemplation.

My approach?

Swaggering, hepcat, ala Hollywood leading-man type, with purpose undisclosed but deadly in earnest, oh most holy earnestness deadly.

My bearing?

North-northeast toward the nicely nicely villainous with due regard for the avoidance of orthodoxish mannerisms.

My bait?

An inconsistent mixture of physical wellbeing, quick, strong, lithe arms prone to violence and by their proximity prone to her.

Also in the mixture?

Desire with a capital D, but desire withheld to a hint, awaiting the proper moment, barely held in check valiantly.

And not to be excluded?

An impression of possession of vast stores of spiritual wares, all hidden, guarded, it being what's up front that counts.

My overall philosophical guide:

These two fundamental axioms: when in doubt, whip it out; and, in other instances, treat the rich girl poorly and the poor girl richly.

Ah ha. In this, friend, we are truly allies, eh what?

To be sure, comrade. In this crotchward endeavor we plan together.

These and other large considerations hurriedly mulled over, he lifted her golden V-shaped spreadeagle and clonked it down. The odds against its being heard mid the rock 'n' roll stampede were overwhelming, he realized, so again he did it to the V-shaped thing, this time harder.

From the other side of the door came her lilting, "Just a minute." Singsonged as: *JUST* a *MIN* it. Nicely nicely.

Quickly the door departed from his listening ear and opened inward, surprisingly quickly, leaving him battling to hide his interrupted listening behind a guise of too much cool-man-cool sauntering.

"Hi. Come in, Dean." She said it with delight, with eyes wide and lips openly spread in a smile of promise, anticipation, everything, including hopefully improper emphasis. It came to him as a sweet melody, came through the din of dissonant rock noise neatly, like a love theme swelling from something rumbling, transitional, and symphonic, swelling up to a flurry.

"Thank you," he said, but with due regard for his planned approach, bearing, guiding philosophy.

She turned her back to him, leaving the door in his care. He closed it quickly. She wore no shoes, toreador pants, tight; sweater, also tight. Her turning presented for his inspection her butt contained in toreadored skin, the small of her back, a delectable valley between butt and back; her back, slender, yet not too slender, sturdy, yet with that willowy flexibility—twisty, an able pivoteer atop spindly waist and ball-and-socket hips. No. Beach ball and air cushion pillow hips. But not only that. She turned, legs spreadeagled at knocker angle, and commenced to do a sort of jog that took her up on her toes, down and up again. But not really up, because her head did not bob. Rather, he discovered from his advantageous view, her knees bent when she went to her toes so that her thighs and butt took up the bounce, keeping her head unbounced. The neat physics of it was outpointed only by the sheer physical grace of it. She did it with quick thrust-bounces. To the music, he suspected, although he couldn't be sure, having abandoned listening to the boom at this point.

He stood watching bouncing Rita, closely watching bouncing Rita, and closely watching, came close to abandoning his guiding philosophy by reaching for her. Rather, by octopussing her and gluing himself to her in preparation for devouring and being devoured, but—

"Oh, man," she moaned happily, "this beat does it. Man, it sends me. You like, I hope?" This she asked leaving on the jog-bounce, jitterbugging like an impassioned Apache, kitchenward. He muttered into the booming rock that he did indeed like it, Amen, and stumblebugged behind her, trying to refuse both the beat of the music and the beat of her bugging. His cool-man-cool attempt at these refusals met with defeat, of course, but he did manage to keep his lips pursed in what he hoped was the proper quality of slight disdain.

"I didn't expect you so soon, Dean," she sang—softly now because the longplay was between numbers momentarily. Sung softly inside the small kitchen, the cozy kitchen, aye, the intimate kitchen: "Anyway, I'm glad you're here. No use you staying over there in your place while I'm only dressing for our date over here, is there? After all."

His respiration hiccuped with agreement so total he could hardly blurt it out and still salvage his attempted cool-man-cool, that being close to inundated anyway now by an urge to grab the bottom of her sweater and the top of her toreadors and, on the count of three, heave apart together.

But, she seemed to have forgotten all about the fact that he might have a reply, any reply, for she was asking him how he liked his highball and would he like to mix them while she showered and dressed. Which she would do, she assured him, with unfeminine dispatch. So, in a trance of utter chaos, he took up the mixing materials she supplied while his mind, heart, and eyes followed her again-jitterbugging body bed-roomward. She turned and smiled her way around the closing bedroom door and he fumbled the cocktail pitcher, caught it, fumbled it, caught it again and wished it were rape-able.

Oh, you lovely beast.

Careful now. Don't rush and ruin. Especially a good thing. Aye, a fantastic, luscious, delicious thing.

Oh dear lord, bless my trigger-happy me. Such a next-door neighbor. Yes, lonely bed, tonight you will be lonelier.

Ah ah, mind your manners. Easy does it. Easy, squeezy, nicely nicely.

The cocktail pitcher in one hand and the bottle of whisky in the other, he took one small step toward the crossing through the living room to the bedroom to the . . . but stopped.

Oh, you beautiful, busty smorgasbord, hear this mental telegraph I now send thee; hear it under your noisy shower cap and through your noisy rock, hear it from tip to stern, entree to main course:

We will, we will, we will. My choice being the simplest of the drugstore devices. Rubber me not, fair maiden; nor parry my thrust with that godawful medical blockade. Squirt the squirt, I pray thee, quickly, when we're done.

How now? Rushing again? Hold that tiger.

He recovered enough to mix the drinks, or something of whisky, ice, and soda pop he hoped would pass for drinks, when he heard the shower cease. They were ready and poured and resting on her fashionably low coffee table in front of her low couch when she emerged, dressed in a party dress, black and pink, low neck exposing swells it barely retained, swells causing swells in him he barely retained. He sat in the only other piece of seating furniture, a wicker chair, and permitted his swelling to her swelling as she, now trucking on high heels to the booming rock again, first went to the kitchen to rinse out the pitcher, then returned to the center of the un-padded couch.

An extrovert, an exhibitionist. And why not, with such wares?

Yes, why not?

"Eue," she squealed, rhyming it with *you* and *cue*, "you mix good drinks. I'll have to get you to mix more."

Many more. Oh, many, many more.

"Absolutely," he said, trying not to mimic her tone, trying for the proper effect, failing.

Must get over the shock of untouched contact. Must divert attention. Think of something else.

"You know where I'd like to go," she said, dropping her head sideways, shifting to a coy, cornering peek.

"Pray tell."

"To the Hamilton Hotel Tea Room."

Good lord! A meal for as much as the government sucks from the paycheck every week! Damn the Joneses! A meal should not cost that much, even for . . . .

Go go go, little tweedy.

"Fine," he said.

Now hear this, fair maiden: honey you're begging for and honey you'll get, at the Hamilton Hotel Tea Room and later. And again and again and again. For you, I got honey that won't quit, Honey. Records shall be broken; worlds shall open to you.

"We could probably walk there," she said.

"Um."

"But I'd rather drive, wouldn't you?"

"Hmm."

"Then I could get out in style and you could park and we could walk in together. That's the way they do it."

"Humph."

"Let's drive?"

"Sure, let's drive."

"You know, they serve the nicest—oh, I don't want to sound like a golddigger. Do I?"

"No, sweetheart, no, You're music to my ears. In fact, you're music to my very root. You're music and poetry in motion, in flesh, in lovely flesh."

"Huh?"

"Nothing. Just mumbling."

"Well?"

"Well what?"

"If you can't afford it, say so."

"Huh?"

"The Hamilton Hotel Tea Room."

"Oh. Sure. We'll drive."

"All right. Now, as I was saying—" The rock selection came to a blaring finale and the needle arm lifted. She toned down to a husky, whispery pseudo. "—As I was saying, they serve the nicest steaks there. Of course, they're expensive." This she tossed out with a gay challenge, one eyebrow lifting.

"Well, why not splurge once in a while. If that's where you want to go," he said loudly and carefully, "that's where we'll go. But remember, you're with a poor Hicksville reporter."

"Oh?" Eyebrow up again.

"Oh. I mean, I don't make wages, like, unionized, like, you dig?"

"Hee hee! You sound so fun-nee."

"Ho ho."

It was two blocks down the street to the Hamilton Hotel.

She wriggled over close beside him and they drove placidly,
listening to the radio people:

      Announcer:
      How would you
      Like to leave your troubles behind
      And fly anywhere
      In the entire free world
      Stop off at the best hotels
      Dine in the most extravagant fashion
      And
      Never
      Pay
      A cent.
      Sound impossible?
      Well it isn't.
      The next time you shop
      Buy a can of Hinklestein's Clam Chowder
      Fill out the coupon
      Which comes with the can
      Of Hinklestein's Clam Chowder
      And mail it.
      You may be the lucky winner
      Of an all-expense-paid
      Luxury vacation
      For two
      Remember
      That's Hinklestein's
      Accept no substitute.

Also, there was news:

      They originally planned to eject the capsule
      and recover it
      by remote control
      as it floated down
      from outer space
      by parachute

The hotel had a small, crowded parking lot behind it. In front was a grand-duchess, doormanned, embarkation point. They drove to the front. She embarked; he parked.

> *Here we go*
> *What a show*
> *Happy music*
> *Happy music*
> *You'll hear the news*
> *While the news is new*
> *Everything's great*
> *On twelve-oh-eight.*

She waited for him in front and they entered through the revolving door, ascended the carpeted staircase to the foyer, proceeded through the lobby to the Tea Room, she with her arm lightly on his arm. He opened for her the glass door to the Tea Room; it made a hissing, puffing comment. The doorman there was temporarily absent. She blossomed forth into the palatial dining room, taking it by storm—historical novel heroine type storm. That is, she stood with chin up, bosom out, derriere pluming, surveying with youthful disdain the interior, seeing nothing, being seen. He stood at her side, surveying with her the surveyors of her, and feeling her superimpose herself, like a dancing nude in a Methodist church, over the tinkling dinner orderliness soaked in music by Muzak. The headwaiter approached, bowed to them, and came up wearing a question directed at Dean. Dean said, "Table for two, please." The headwaiter dropped his eyebrows, executed a swooping turn, and went with lunging strides over the cushioned carpeting to a small table in the corner farthest from the door. The eyes of their elders and financial betters upon them, they followed, she behind the headwaiter, he behind her noisy, metronoming taffeta bustle. The headwaiter bowed her into her chair in the corner and asked, in accordance with his precise sense of orderliness, if they would prefer something to drink before ordering.

"No, thank you," said Dean as she drew a preparatory breath. The headwaiter was immediately replaced by his successor, the waiter, who presented menus, large, stiff, slick-papered menus with prices tactfully withheld for the benefit of madame's cause. They sat staring at their menus for a moment.

Note the orderliness, my friend.

Orderliness to the point of chaos.

Class, my friend, class.

Class for this ass?

For this classy ass.

A jumble of the appurtenances of class, a chaos.

Oh no. The utmost in reasonability, in sane and elegant cannibalistic vegetarianism. From the cushioning to the chandeliers and around the warm wormwood hung with imitation eighteenth-century purples, blood reds, browns, blues, burnished yellows.

My tasty young she-in-heat in this?

Certainly. Improving it, too.

This it could stand, but—

Improving the dinner-tinkle by her lively inner-tinkle.

Impossible. She sits on her brains, thank God.

The tinkle, my friend, comes from her she, not her brains, thank God.

Okay. Uncle.

"It's nice here, isn't it," she exploded, dropping her menu, staring about.

"A neat, well-lighted padded cell," he said. "Quite nice."

"Oh, *you!* Hee hee hee. You say the fun-nee-ist things."

"Ho ho."

"Hey." She shot this at him with a forward thrust of her head. "Did you hear about that murder?" It started as a question and ended as a declaration, followed by "Eue, the maniacs there are around here!"

"I—"

"Gee, I get scared all over just thinking."

Yes.

Tut tut.

"You should have seen—" he again attempted.

"Imagine! What would make a person *do* a thing like that? What did *she* ever do? A mother!"

"I," he said, bulling his way through, "was the first reporter at the scene."

Such tactics, it seems, are necessary.

Attaboy.

"Oh, how dumb do you think I am," she chided.

Pretty damn.

Tut tut.

She giggled. "You *never!* Expect me to believe *that?* I heard you this morning. I can hear you from my place. Don't kid *me*, mister."

But but but—

Remember, my friend, we are presently engaged in the means, not the ends; and also that the better part of valor and all that, and the brick wall and the easiest way through—or in—is over.

He shrugged. "Well, I was there. At dawn."

"Were you? I mean, really?"

"Sure."

"Eue!"

"Should have seen her."

"Eue! What was she like?"

"Nude."

"I mean, *you* know."

"Nice."

"Eue!"

"But with a hatchet in her head, her frontal lobe."

"Eue!"

"Bloody. Very bloody."

"Let's not talk about it."

"With her clothes torn and pulled off."

"Eue!"

"Murdered and raped."

"Oh, *good*ness! How *dread*ful! Eue!"

Hot damn, baby doll, I'll have you by the Id in no time.

Careful, careful. Watch your timing. The repercussion of conscience must come as you leave, not as you approach.

"Horrible." He shook his head and lowered his chin.

"A girl just isn't safe at all these days, is she."

"Not with maniacs like that running loose."

"Eue! It sends chills all *through* me, and goose bumps, *too*."

"They'll catch him."

"Oh yes. They *have* to."

"It may be somebody local, too. Somebody who'd know about her, maybe somebody who knew her pretty well."

"Eue!"

"Yes, that's my hunch."

Wow! Spread so thickly?

Certainly. The thicker the better. Communication being a two-way proposition, the code used must be immediately understood by both sender and receiver, a phenomenon, as you know, well known by *we* mass media senders.

Send ho!

"Do they have any idea who *did* it; I mean, who *really* did?"

"Oh, they have a list of suspects."

"Gee! Who's the one they suspect most?"

He laughed. "Oh, that would be talking out of school."

"Ah, tell me, come on, please. I won't tell, honest."

"All right. Brace yourself; this will come as a surprise."

"Who?"

"Me."

"Eue! Hee hee hee. You're awful!"

"Well, they've picked up a few guys. It'll be in the paper tomorrow."

"But tell me tonight."

"Okay. Tonight."

"No, you know what I mean. *Now!*"

"Now?"

"Come on, who did they pick up?"

"I'm out on bond."

"Oh, don't be silly," she pouted.

"Well, it's like this: if I told you and you told somebody else, and they told somebody else, and it got around town, the next time there was anything to tell, I wouldn't be told anything."

She looked hurt. "But I *said* I wouldn't tell."

"Yes, but it's the principle of the thing. After all, I have to be true to myself, don't I?"

She sighed and returned to her menu. The waiter returned to their table and they ordered steaks.

She forgot her curiosity quickly enough and turned to a jitterbugging jibberjabber about life behind the counter in the department store. While responding as her tone demanded, responding adequately, mechanically, his mind slinked away to the footpath and the red and white cottage at midmorning. From there, it followed Mrs. Donaldson's pink nude remains to the autopsy table where, he estimated, it now was. He declined to follow the probing surgical blade past an initial incision. And the steaks arrived just as Rita was becoming indignant about a proposition hint dropped by a floorwalker. They cut their meat and ate, mostly in silence, and when they finished the meal, he paid and they left, unaccompanied by either headwaiter or doorman.

She waited at the embarkation point in front while he fetched a singing chorus of rolling radio people.

> *Wherever you go*
> *There is radio,*
> *In your car*
> *near or far*
> *always there is radio.*

He rounded the corner and found her standing with chin up and legs sassy, fashion-model-wise, slightly behind and to the left of the uniformed doorman, near a dowager waiting for her chauffeur. The unhappy condition and vintage of his car as it approached did not seem to break her spell.

Ah ha! Muzak-soaked, steak-stuffed.

Proceed. Big round coming up.

Yes, bringing up an important question: to move in for a quick take, or spar for a smooth make?

Consider last night's encounter, oh great one, and also our axiom, and exercise control.

How much control?

Much more than last night.

Well, of course.

But not so much that you become absurd by breaching the boundaries of accepted absurdity. Align thyself with her expectations, coincide with that absurdity. Respond to her cue.

She doth, too, cue.

That she doth. But soft, soft, ever aware of our axiom: the poor girl richly.

That axiom, my wallet tells me, is now suspect. But there are certain pitfalls, no matter. . . .

The doorman, being dowager-distracted, disdained to open the door of Dean's old car for her. Dean popped out, rounded the front bumper gallantly and, despite a part of himself, opened the door for her, absurding to that absurdity, maintaining her spell.

The radio people again, as they drove placidly, shelled them.

Chorus:
No matter where you have to go
It helps you if you know
The time, the correct time
(Sound of Chinese gong.)

Announcer:
It's now seven o'clock
Time to hear
From America's
Producers of milk.
One of the blessings
of living in
modern America
is high quality
nourishing milk....

That commercial's end brought this song:

Everybody likes to cha cha cha
Little children like to cha cha cha

"What's on at the drive-in?" she chirped.
"Augh! Just westerns," he lied. "Nothing good."
"I like westerns, don't you?"
"Oh, sure. I like them best on television."
"I like them in the movies once in awhile."
"Once in awhile, but I like to just sit home."
"You know what happened *last* night."
"Yes. Nothing."
"Nothing!" She giggled. "You didn't behave yourself, *that's* what."
"I fell victim to your overwhelming charms, Sweet Reet."
"Said the spider to the fly."
"What's this spider-fly bit? I'm not trying to trap you."
At which point, he received support from the radio:

Baby, if you'll let me take you by the hand
I'm gonna teach this dance to you

"Don't be nasty." This said with snide sweetness. Then she burst into a rapture, okaying by subject and presentation the stay-home, the second chapter: "Eue, don't they make the nicest steaks there!"
"Yes. Well, they don't exactly make them there."

"Oh don't be silly. They do so."

"May I beg to differ? The steaks come from animals, butchered for us to eat, butchered, maybe, in Chicago."

"Eue, you make it sound bloody."

Everybody likes to cha cha cha

"Sorry."

"Anyway, they were good. Cooked good."

"Yeah."

"I think," she exubed, turning to watch his expression, "it calls for a drink."

He sighed contentedly. "I'm in complete and utter agreement, Sweet Reet."

Then—anonymity being difficult and in some vague way required—she preceded him into the apartment building while he cruised in search of a place to park the car, a tacitly made agreement against the whom and whatever. When he arrived, her door was open a crack and drinks were being poured in large water glasses on her low coffee table. He slipped out of his jacket, loosened his necktie and slumped down on the couch, watching her frisk back to the kitchen to replace the whisky and mix instead of leaving it for a much simpler mixing of follow-ups in the living room. He enjoyed watching her move clickingly over the linoleum floor, and she, by the patterns and movements she made, enjoyed his enjoying. She returned, plopped down beside him, lifted her glass and slyly proposed: "To Dean, who wants more than he can have."

"I won't drink to that," he proclaimed, banging his drink down on her table.

"Why not?" she giggled.

"Because I don't think it's true."

"Oh? And what do you mean by that?"

"It's dishonestly pessimistic."

"Eue! You conceited thing, you!"

Silence.

"Well?" she asked, still hoisting her glass.

"Here's to contact," he said softly, lifting his.

"Contact!" An exclamation of horror.

"Yes, contact."

She admonished him with a giggle. "You're bad."

"No, you don't understand."

"Oh no?"

"No. By contact I mean that we, you and I, shall fuse, become one, communicate, send and receive on the same frequency."

"Sounds crazy." She lifted her glass higher. "Crazy, man."

They touched glasses and sipped.

    Attaboy.

    I thought so, too.

"Hey, let's spin one." She bounded up, clicked to her phonograph, and spun one. And performed to the opening bars.

> *There is something on your mind*
> *. . . By the way you look at me.*
> *There is something on your mind, honey*
> *. . . By the way you look at me.*
> *Can what you're thinking*
> *Bring happiness:*
> *Or will it bring . . . misery.*
> *No, please don't try to tell me*
> *I think I understand*
> *No . . . no don't have to tell me, pretty baby,*
> *. . . I think I understand.*

He joined her and they danced.

    Easy, chief, it's early yet.

    Easy is easy in all this taffeta.

    She'll soon fix that.

    Tit for tat.

    Prepare thyself, tat.

When the number ended and he spun her around ball-roomishly and murmured in her ear, "Hmm, you smell delicious, Sweet Reet," she spun out of his loose encircling arms and twirled her way bedroomward.

"Be out in a minute," she sang on the twirl.

He huffed at his frustration and slumped back on the couch in front of his drink. For something to do he tasted his drink, then tasted hers. He estimated that his had about three times as much whisky.

She plays it well, this tit for tat.

Agreed. I'm breathless. But she wants more tat than I can safely give for her tit.

Quite so.

Even if I could safely pay her price, I'd be obliged, the old ball game being what it is, to try for more for less.

Yes, yes. More for less, that's the game.

Hence, lacking an abundance of tat, I must set my sights on getting more tit for less tat, on getting more of her for less of me.

Ah, such fantastically sound reasoning! In this, Ally, we agree utterly.

Thus far in the ball game, however, I'm afraid I've been outscored.

Indeed, my friend, this pains me more than it does you.

So, we must study the situation, define our position and prepare for the moment of truth.

Yes, yes, for the moment of truth.

First, the object:

Plainly, copulation.

The reason:

There ain't no reason. It's the policy.

Ingredients:

Simply a matter of vaginal secretions and blood displacement—would that more were necessary—rendered into manifest being by the proper improper stimuli.

Improper stimuli?

For you, no problem. For her, your problem. May I suggest?

By all means.

Then, since she is attempting to suggest, obviously hoping to outpoint you again, you might become wrapped up in something else, providing her suggesting with the opposition of your distracted attention; then she will be forced to relinquish certain ground gained by suggestion to recapture attention, and as she relinquishes, you pursue, filling every opening as she makes openings available for filling, until—

Ally, compatriot, friend, comrade, buddy! You delight me with your innate wisdom. But, pray tell, what might I use for this mousetrap play?

The box, my friend, the box. Flip the switch, I tell you, and unplug that siren, the phonograph— *her* tool.

Ah, yes, television. The news. Far from her inverted V in motion my mind will appear to wander when over the seas, snooping through Europe, Russia, India, China, peeking up the newsy nostril of her receiving box I go.

Lights, camera, action!

In the proper sequence.

He turned off her phonograph, turned on her television, and turned off the floor lamp beside the couch, just in time for the seven-thirty news.

The tubes spoke thusly:

And now when my boy needs a laxative
I never have to coax him
He takes flavored Phillips willingly
And likes it so much he even asks for more.
And I don't blame him.
It's really amazing how good Phillips works.

Then the other people told him that John Foster Dulles had resigned and the president had been seen with a tear trickling down his cheek, an emotional matter, news wrapped thusly:

> Those who admire John Foster Dulles
> as well as those who do not
> will have several reasons to regret
> that his health did not allow him to carry on.
> The first
> and obvious reason is that some important
> and maybe critical meetings with Russia
> are about to begin.

At this point, Sweet Reet Rita Helwig arrived with her heavenly hellwiggle again toreadored. She stepped forth from the bedroom, hands on hips, coy smile partly flooded by a frown, and surveyed with hunched shoulders and tilted head his television news viewing, which continued:

> It may be that nobody in the west is
> really prepared for them
> but
> if anyone is
> it's Dulles.
> Another reason is this:
> He had the utter
> total
> complete confidence of the president
> and therefore
> a greater freedom of action than any other
> secretary of state
> in modern history.
> He used his freedom to make
> American
> foreign policy.
> He made it
> sometimes without telling anyone else
> what it was.

And if
maybe
while he was shaving he changed his mind
he changed the policy.
No successor could have this degree of
confidence and freedom
so
the next secretary
will step into what amounts to a one-man
department of state
without
the one man.
It was difficult enough with Dulles.
Without him
it may be more so.

"Hey," chirped Rita, "what happened to the music?"

"It quit. I knocked it off. I want to hear the news."

"What for?" She marched toward the box.

"Wait!"

"What for?"

"About the murder. You want to hear about the murder, don't you?"

"Eue." She drew back, half turned and crab-walked with her eyes on the set to her place beside him.

From the box came a swell of violin music, neo-symphonic and ultra sweet. Then, the announcer appeared and said:

New

Then the music swelled again; then the announcer said:

Deluxe

Then the music gushed up to a sweet, heartrending crescendo, a climax of extraordinary sensuality; then it cascaded down, like fresh, gentle waters from a secret mountain spring over mossy rocks into a glistening inlet resplendent with soft, tropical growth, and the announcer said:

America's first deluxe cake mixes
Duncan Hines deluxe
Inspired by Duncan Hines

Meanwhile the box showed different angles of a cake attended by a model, who smiled seductively. The cake spun on its axis and the music swelled again into another orgiastic gush, and the announcer said:

America's authority on good eating.
A new discovery for you
cake you couldn't serve till now
here's yellow cake with a deluxe secret
a moisture miracle that brings you
tender
moist
texture.

Then the music swelled still yet again as the video cut to the sexy cake model with a knife in her hand. She sank the knife into the cake and smiled at the camera as if she were with a highly satisfying lover who had just completed one issue of his passion and was preparing to deliver another.

The announcer, meanwhile, continued in a soft voice off-camera as if he were the lover of the smiling, knife-wielding cake model.

Cuts
at a touch.

The music zoomed up again.

Moist delicious layers

And cascaded down to become background again.

Lavishly made with finest ingredients
even to specially selected vanillas
every morsel
plump with moisture

The violins yawned impishly.

> to bring out all the mellow flavors.
> Only deluxe yellow cake
> with the moisture miracle
> has such golden richness.
> Look for America's first and only deluxe cake mixes
> in new luxury size packages.
> Serve new Duncan Hines deluxe yellow cake
> tomorrow.

Then the other announcer came upon the tubes once more and said:

> In Ridiculee Township today
> a young
> attractive
> widow was brutally murdered
> by a sex maniac.

Then through the tubes came the scene—the Donaldson home, the tangle of people and cars crammed into the cinder-and-mud clearing.

> The murdered woman
> was Mrs. Sara Donaldson
> widow of a promising
> young attorney who died last November.
> She had a four-year-old son
> who was in the house
> at the time of the murder
> but is too young
> for police to question.
> As these shots
> taken at the scene shortly after
> the murder was discovered show
> the insanity of the crime

brought hundreds of shocked
and distraught neighbors rushing to the scene.
There have been murders before
and will be again
no doubt
but this one
because its victim was a young widow
who had suffered the tragedy of her husband's death
only last year
and because
it was so unreasonably brutal and fiendish
is particularly shocking.
It's the worst anyone in Ridiculee
can recall
ever being committed
in their suburban and rural
township.
The Donaldson home
is in a semi-rural section
heavily wooded
and sparsely populated.
Police were busy all day
combing the woods
for traces of the killer
and questioning a large number of suspects
and
no doubt
preparing to arrest
known sex deviates
in the town-
township and district.

Reet got in an "Eue!" as the announcer paused for the
camera to catch him at a three-quarter angle before continuing
with a short life history of Mrs. Donaldson. Then the tubes
cut to a wire service photograph of her face taken from a

living room photograph; it was unflattering and Rita lost interest.

She departed from the couch after her short visit there and crouched neatly before her collection of records for a bit of research leading to a selection. Then, softly behind the announcer's chatter, came other sounds:

> *Tippy, tippy, tippy toe*
> *Out my window I will go*
> *Cause, Sweetheart, I love you so*
> *Tippy, tippy, tippy toe!*

Over this, the television people were saying:

> . . . and in Hoboken
> a forty-six-year-old minister
> W. W. Winthrop
> has admitted stealing tools
> from a school
> and a garage.

Meanwhile, Rita had started to dance to her phonograph music. The new costume she wore was suited quite well to her expressionistic solo—a loose slipover sweater, tight at points; black toreadors, altogether tight without points; no shoes. Her hip-swaying caused the loose bottom of the jersey to sway and her knee-bending bouncing flexed the toreadors even tighter at times and in places.

Dean leaned toward the box and frowned at it. He was much aware of her movements from the corner of his eye but pretended to be concentrating on the talking tubes.

As she danced, she held her arms up and outstretched toward him and contorted her face into a squinting, open-mouthed silent cry of mad ecstasy.

Eue, man, eue!

Not yet.

Her music-maker said:

> *Trying not to make a sound*
> *Tippy, tippy toe*
> *Come on, baby, let me know*

His tube people said:

> Wait
> lady wait.
> That's the wrong way to add bleach to the wash.
> Don't you know
> that just guessing when you wash
> can cause damage to your hubby's clothes. . . .

And her music-maker said:

> *Out my window I will go*
> *Cause, Sweetheart, I love you so*

And so it went.

As her next record began, he rose and went to the tubes and switched to a new station. Its hero, a dapper fellow said:

> I respected Mr. Watkins,
> He gave me my first break.

And a pretty heroine answered:

> That's the way I feel about him
> too.
> Do you really think
> he's capable.

The hero frowned and pursed his lips and said:

> Of murder?

The heroine, face tilted up coquettishly, said:

> Yes
> the murder of
> his associate.

The hero paused, giving the matter anguished consideration, possibly appealing silently to certain metaphysical beings, then said:

> Not unless he
> had a motive.

Dean switched to another station and found two western-type fellows stationed on an outdoor set. The first said:

> Used to be plenty of water.
> Then them minin' fellers come along
> built ditches up above here
> took water that was rightfully ourn.
> Now us farmers
> can barely eke out a livin'.

The second fellow, speaking around a tooth-picking weed, said:

> Seems hard to believe

Dean switched again. Progressive jazz supporting a trombone solo, accompanying a female vocalist, standing at three-quarter angle, rocking and humming to the music.

> Basso male voice off:
> You can always tell a girl
> with a maidenform musicmaker
> the bra with class . . .

Then he switched off the television, went to her phonograph, and turned up its volume, caught her dainty right hand in his left hand and applied his right hand to the small of her back, to the flexing of her dancing back. They danced, she to recorded music, he to her dancing sinews and his own choreographic ambitions. Ambitious choreographer that he was, his hand soon danced its way to contact with the smooth bare skin of the small of her performing back.

"Eue Dean!" It was a gay, up-the-scale scolding he ignored, except to check temporarily his initial exploration.

"Oh Dean." This came down the scale.

They danced to:

> *Slightly slimmer than a fishing pole*
> *One half rock and one half roll*

"Eue," she squealed as they executed a series of steps which pleased her.

> *Dig that chick from either side*
> *Man, you'll yell, "Where did she hide"*

"And you said you weren't a good dancer."

> *Skinny Minnie?*
> *She ain't skinny*
> *She's tall*
> *That's all*

His right hand, fetched by the lure of unexplored bare back, crept upward.

"Dean." Again up the scale.

> *What there ain't*
> *That's what she be*

But where the groping pioneers, his fingers, expected to encounter an equator of cloth and lastex where such an equator is customarily presumed to exist, he found none.

"Dean." Back down again.

> *Skinny Minnie*
> *She ain't skinny*

He applied an enveloping pressure which brought her torso to his torso.

"Eue Dean." Up and down the scale.

And he felt the tight parts of her jersey squash like puffy melons against his ribs, then roll as they danced.

She's tall
That's all

This pressed deflation caused a pressing inflation.

Tisk, tisk. You're rushing, my friend.

Your friend is rushing me, mighty ally.

Quite so, but you're the boss of this outfit, aren't you?

I like to think so, but—

Then be the boss; demand more for less not less for more. Play the game, my friend.

Yes, but—

Oh, don't think I don't understand your predicament. I understand all too well.

Well, if anybody should, you should.

But does she?

Certainly.

I mean, will she admit to understanding?

Your question, compatriot, will be answered immediately following this whirl and dip.

Whoopee!

"Dean, you're not behaving."

"Not behaving?"

"No. Remember what we agreed last night?"

"Humph."

"Well?"

"Sweet Reet, it's you, I can't help it. You do this to me. I can't *help* it."

"Oh, can't help it my eye."

Quite so. See how her eye can't help it?

Yes yes, I see. Quite encouraging.

Quite. Proceed.

"Eue, don't do that! I can't *stand* to be kissed there. It gives me *goose* bumps."

"Umm."

"Now stop it."

"Umm."

"Dean, *please!* Eue golly gee, this is *only* our second *date!*"
Statistics!
Eue golly-gee-gadzooks!
Profanity!

"Eue."

"Umm."

"Eue! Dean Dean Dean!"

"Umm."

She's relaxing.
Follow through, hero, and good luck.
Damn those toreadors! I'd almost prefer the panty girdle obstacle nearly surmounted last night.
Never say die, et cetera. Especially with her will on the wane pointing the way.
Is she?
Breathing? Certainly, and quickly.
Yes, and with passion.
With teetertottering.
Has her teeter tottered?
Surely it's nearing a tottering.
Is her waning gaining?
Surely it's turning.
Will she compromise her more for less for my less for more.
Neatly it curtsies.
Must ride this momentum.
Must indeed, and not only that.
Yes.
All yesses?
Yes.
Charge! Onward to the fray, or more precisely, the couch. Horizont the vertical. Trod the uplifted and uplift the downtrodden. Go, man, go.

"Dean?" Softly in a rush of breath, up the scale to a question.

Oh mighty melonous mammilla:
  I salute thee: eue and eue.
Oh snug toreadors:
  Where art thy zipper?
"Eue Dean."
  A zipper hunt, a zipper hunt, we're going on a zipper hunt.

Ah ah! Function, hero, with cool decorum, according to her sense of propriety, not according to your heat and tendency, ever cognizant of the goal we must achieve by indirect stealth. X marks the spot.

Here we are.

Zip zip, quick quick.

Oh Sweet Reet, to touch the tender you of your shanks and flanks is more than this erupting me of mine can stand.

Don't stop! Don't, don't stop.

Ayeee, I can't. This whirlpool takes me as if its force had no other purpose. I'm no longer me but a twig in the rush and thunder of this delicious Rita's luscious Hellwig.

Oh flange, Sweet Reet.

Yes, and quickly.

Eureka!

Her moans rose, then changed to an insistent series of yelps. Then, with shocking suddenness, she slapped him—the last thing he now expected—and, tugging up her tugged down toreadors, wriggled out from under him and ran stumbling into her bedroom and slammed the door shut behind her.

The lady's in her box.

And the box is in the lady.

And a box tells the lady what to do.

And not to do.

There was lots of lubrication.

An abundance of sensation.

Then what, pray tell, caused her to bolt and run?

Instead of—?

A transgressing lubrication versus orthodox persuasion.

Holy evil versus happy guilt.

Transgression on the skid bumps into blocks of blah.

Protagonists in conflict with protagonists—shadow-boxers all.

Immoral immorality against that mockery of morals, that negative laid down by scabby ancestors: Thou Shalt Not.

Ah, hero, answer this: does your voltage fed by her voltage not transcend that obsolete venereal negative?

Yes.

Then, happy horrors, Thou Shalt!

That maniac!

Oh yes you are.

That maniac?

Certainly. Obviously. Most assuredly.

Oh no. That maniac is held in check by me.

Tut tut. Such psychopathic egoism!

He slumped panting and lay prone on her couch. A torrent of despair washed him, but the despair was partly guilt, partly hopelessness, partly anger, partly defeat; he found himself floundering between a militant insistence to act, to storm into her bedroom, to take her, force her, and an equally strong feeling of tired defeat which begged him to leave her apartment, forget her, forget his mad lust for her, to douse his desire with the cold beer of denatured reason.

But before he could get his breath back, the bedroom door opened again and she streamed out, crying. She flung herself on the floor by the couch, pressed her face against his ribs and sobbed.

Must I?

What else?

He smoothed her hair and patted her shoulder and asked, "What's the matter, honey?" Tonelessly, half-hearted pretense.

Egads.

Egads nothing. Your role in this phase of the little drama. Play it to the hilt. Pull out all stops and go, man, go.

"Baby, don't cry. I'm sorry. I guess I just got carried away."

Her voice choked with sobs and thick with crying, she wailed, "What kind of a girl do you think I am?"

This is too much!

No no. Don't let up. Stick in there. That, after all, is an encouraging question.

Encouraging? A leading question, yes. Leading like the smell of cheese in a very old trap.

Not necessarily, my friend, a steel trap.

Hmm.

Carry on. She awaits your silly reply to her silly question. Silly-ho!

"Ah, Sweetheart, don't cry, please. I can't stand it."

Oh what the hell! Why don't we stop this idiotic claptrap and copulate.

Ah ah! Play the game, hero. Her move.

"Well, I—sob—can't help it. Hic. After all, I'm not some slut you picked up off the street."

Would that you were!

"Honey, forgive me. I can't help it either. You do things to me. I know you don't *mean* to, but—"

Yike! That's too much.

No no. To the hilt, to the hilt.

"But, well, you do," he continued. "You're so beautiful, I can't help myself. I just get carried away."

"You seem to think you're the only one with feelings. Sob-hic. What about me? Ooh-hooooo!"

"Ah, honey."

"You think I don't have feelings, that I don't feel, too?

Humph! Hic. Well, I do. After all, I'm only human, too, you know. But what if I'd let myself go: what would you think of me then?"

Eue, Sweet Reet!

Hush. Let the lady continue.

"You'd just . . . I'd be just . . . it would be all *over*."

"Oh no, Baby, no, no."

"Oh don't give me that. I know. I've seen it happen. To other girls, I mean. Not me. Sob. I'm not that kind."

Ugh!

Stick in there, hero.

"Honey, it's all my fault. There, I've said it and I'm sorry. I mean *glad!* But, then, it's not *all* my fault. You—you're . . . I just can't help myself."

"Well, you'd better help yourself. Hiccup!"

Eue.

Eue eue.

Her sobs subsided. "I do like you, Dean. In fact," she said carefully, "I'm *fond* of you."

"I wish you were half as fond of me as I am of you."

She hid a smile. "Oh please! You don't mean that. All you want—"

"Is you, Rita."

"Humph." She nestled her head against his arm.

Attaboy.

Oh? Who won?

No one, but you didn't lose, for a change. It's now Love and your serve, but this time, slam for point without knocking the ball over the fence.

This time may never come. I'm tired. I'm up a tree and out on a limb and bushed.

She purred: "Let's dance." Her pensive mask was not entirely successful.

A new record had just dropped:

> *You must remember this*
> *A kiss is still a kiss*

They danced slowly, sedately, with her head loosely on his shoulder and his right arm limply around her waist, their feet moving slightly, bodies not touching. But, occasionally, bumping.

"You know, Dean," she said, scolding sweetly, "what happens whenever you get like that."

"Like what?"

"Oh . . . you know. You know what I mean."

"Who knows? I don't know a thing, especially about you, Sweet Reet."

They bumped. Then she bumped. Then he bumped.

> *And when two lovers woo*
> *They still say, "I love you"*

"Oh, Dean. . . .

"Now, Dean, please! . . .

"Dean?"

"Umm."

"Dean, when this is over, why don't you go back to your place and change into something comfortable."

"My birthday suit?"

"Eue. Hee hee hee. Don't be sil-lee. . . .

"Now stop that, Dean!

"*Dean!*"

> *Woman needs man*
> *And man must have his mate*

"I really think we should separate, for awhile, so you can get those silly notions out of your head."

"I don't want to separate, Sweet Reet. I like my silly notions."

"Eue. . . .

"Dean, I warned you. Now *stop!* . . .

"Dean, I don't like what's happening. Eue. I'm warning you. Now just stop it, right now! No. Eue. Stop it. Eue, please!"

And when two lovers woo
They still say, "I love you"

"All right! Damn it, you win. I quit. I'm leaving. Won't be back." He grabbed his suit jacket from the couch, strode past her as she watched wide-eyed and open-mouthed, and left, slamming her front door behind him most satisfactorily and louder than she had slammed her bedroom door behind her.

Enough's enough.

Attaboy.

The next is up to her.

At's the spirit.

She could drive a guy mad, pushing herself against him and with no bra and all.

Especially all.

Yes, so there's only one thing to do.

On beer?

It will take a lot of beer, but—

Barward ho!

Away from dripping rock and roll.

Away from dripping Rita.

Away from dripping.

Away, away!

In quest of?

A gin-soaked bag, a hunching hag, the losers of the game; till death us part from this cruel mart, this giggling at the pain. It's Rita-made and will invade the most unsavory Jane.

It's all the same.

Down the hall, out the door, along the sidewalk toward the corner bar went Dean, toward the noise and smoke.

A Stranger in Grand Central Station

He wondered as he pushed open the heavy wooden door to the bar if he would find Mark the poet. If Mark were there, he would be found standing at the bar with one foot resting on the brass rail and one hand holding a bottle of beer. He would be wearing a teeshirt, jeans, loafers. His shaggy, self-barbered hair would be creeping up his neck to a thick, uncombed tangle on top. His face would be reflected in the mirror behind the bar and would seem unresponsive, turned inside out, coarse yet childlike, seemingly unaware of all the noise around him and keenly aware of the noise within himself.

The noise was a constant stream of human wailing, as if everyone at once was bemoaning the moment and calling for tomorrow. But it was not a completely sad wailing. It was a resigned, what-the-hell wailing, the wailing of everyone who accepted the policy, paid the insurance company, and didn't ask why there was no reason.

Mark would be standing in the midst of and with all this, happily asking unanswerable questions. His happiness would wear a sad mask and would be the sadness of one who is unable to pay the insurance company because he asks why there is no reason, why no reality other than that conjured from the manifestations of the mystery. Nevertheless, it would be a happiness despite its sad mask, happy because it would be asking, always asking. Mark had to be asking in order to live and Dean had to ask Mark, find out from Mark what questions Mark had been asking lately.

But Mark wasn't there. All sorts of people were there, wearing happy masks, in booths along the wall to his left as he entered and standing at the bar to his right. The lights were colored and the what-the-hell wailing was loud; it had to be loud to drown out the television set, blaring down at one and all from its throne at the far end above the bar. The wailing came from all sorts of people—a quartet of young ladies waiting, trying to resolve *that* paradox; a line of young gentlemen standing at the bar, well dressed, by their stance and demeanor paying homage to *that* king of kings; a group of sport-shirted, jacketed millworkers, banded together loosely at the end of the bar under the television set to silently roar their illusionary proclamation in the teeth of the wailing; a pair of middle-aged matrons in search of lost youth's mask of contempt; a pair of middle-aged gentlemen, maybe college instructors, ignoring the general wailing by creating their own island of more harmonic wailing. But Mark wasn't there.

Dean ordered a glass of beer for a dime from the bartender, who wormed his way through the midst of it all wearing a white apron.

Then Dean silently addressed Mark, who wasn't there.

How's the writing going, said Dean. Okay, said Mark, except that there's no money in it. Don't, said Dean, be bitter. Poetry readers are respectable people, well fed and all, and don't need poetry. The thing is, said Mark, nobody likes to be disturbed. Do you like to be disturbed. No, said Dean, and I've just been disturbed by a huge negation, my next-door neighbor. A huge negation over a very positive attraction. That, said Mark, is a shame. I, said Dean, think so too. I, said Mark, read your story in the newspaper, the one about who is the maniac responsible. Did you, said Dean, like it. No, said Mark. I know why you didn't, said Dean. You didn't like it because it wants to know who, not why. That's right, said

Mark. I know, said Dean, but you can't go asking questions like *why*—not out loud, in public. You know that. Yes, said Mark, I know. That's why I quit the game and started concentrating on poetry. You can ask all sorts of questions in poetry and you can also make discoveries, if you're lucky. That, said Dean, is nice. Anyway, I hear a reporting job is about to open up on the paper. Do you want it. Tell me, said Mark, are they looking for a crime specialist, someone to dish up more of that nice, juicy, succulent, tenderized feast for all the would-be rapists and murderers. Do they want a cliché manipulator to give them enough for their mind's teeth to sink into, bite off, chew, savor, censor and drain out all the delicious blood of it and bring the senses to bear on the delicate flavor of it—hatchet in skull, sexually assaulted. Sexually. Now there's a word, a word to be rolled about, begun by a kiss of the tongue and the mouth's roof, climaxed by puckering lips reaching for a nipple, and finally ended by a kittenish half-smile. Well, said Dean, you must admit that at least it's a fashionable word. Yes, said Mark, because it has enough syllables. If, said Dean, you want the job on the paper, you can have it. I, said Mark, don't want it. My only satisfaction would be in feeding the morbid interest of the morbid respectable, and it would be a shallow satisfaction, very shallow. My trouble is that I have no interest in compounding the compounded absurdity. It would be too much like riding a rollercoaster which never stopped. I'd become dizzy and sick and would want to get off, and yet I'd also be laughing so hard at myself I wouldn't want to, and couldn't anyway because I'd be going so fast. What, said Dean, would you laugh at. What would you find so amusing about that which you hated. Morbid interest, said Mark. That's always amused me. For instance, see that dapper fellow at the other end of the bar, reading your story of the Donaldson murder. Notice how absorbed he is, how spellbound. Are you responsible for binding that spell. Is it your skill as a weaver of words which holds him. Certainly not. Yes, said Dean, I know it's not. It's his own morbid interest in the rape and murder, of course. But, said Mark, are you able to imagine the force of all the morbid interest in the world if it were directed at once in the same direction at the same object. No, said Dean, that's beyond me. It's like trying to imagine infinity. That's right, said Mark, but even if we can't imagine it, we can toy with the symbols of an imagining of it. So, just for fun, let's toy. Now the first thing we need is an object. Suppose we take the Donaldson woman and focus the world's attention on the rape and murder of her, arousing Mr. Morbid Interest's compulsion for both procreation and destruction, and concentrating them on one object, one combination, one rape-murder. What do we have. I suppose, said Dean, we have everyone torn to shreds in one ambivalent gasp. Maybe, said Mark, I don't know. But in order to disguise chaos, let us place between the bare acts a hierarchy of symbols which grow out of the bare acts. So that we now have worship of the symbols which, ultimately, have derived from rape and murder. Now what do we have. Ah, said Dean, yes, I see. Now we have law and order. Well, said Mark, a human law and order. An absurd law and order, said Dean. We, said Mark, can only conclude that a man is a very fertile cannibal who sustains himself by killing his own in order to re-create his kind. He rarely kills quickly, because that's not the civilized way. Mostly he kills slowly, gradually, artfully, according to law. Are you, said Dean, trying to say that the rape-murder of the Donaldson woman is a synthesis of human existence. There you go, said Mark, trying to synthesize and simplify. I was only investigating the human predicament symbolically. I offer no theories or maxims. I arrive at a conclusion, a paradox, but my arrival is based on an imaginary situation, a concentration of consciousness, symbolically, which may or may not be considered fitting for lack of reasons. But whether or not it fits our sense of the real, I think it sheds light on the things which I wished to shed light on, for your sake—that we angels are devils and couldn't be unless we were. Shades,

said Dean, of Freud. And, said Mark, of Christ, Marx, and
many others, including that guy at the bar, still avidly reading your account of the rape and murder. Well, said Dean,
maybe you have something there. Let's tune in on that guy
and hear what he has to say about it.

GUY

(At the end of the bar, hereafter referred to as
MORBID INTEREST, *caught at this moment quite un-*
aware of DEAN's *interest)*

Tisk, tisk, tisk.

DEAN

Peekaboo, I see you, hiding behind your tisk-tisk-tisk. Don't
try to hide. I know you're there. I see you, Morbid Interest.
You're so nicely hidden most of the time, but your appetite
is what gave you away today. Papers sold like crazy. Such
an appetite. Tisking and sucking in the life-giving mayhem
manure which keeps you alive and kicking and excreting the
nicest little thrillers for the entertainment of your fellow man.
Oh yes, you are a benevolent censor, aren't you. Such a jolly
cycle you perpetuate.

MORBID INTEREST

You say something, pal?

DEAN

Say something! I've been prattling on and on while you
wallowed in that sloppy gore I wrote.

MORBID INTEREST

Huh?

DEAN

Never mind. What's the use?

MORBID INTEREST

What's that? You'll have to speak up, pal.

DEAN

I say, do you find that story you're reading interesting?

MORBID INTEREST

Certainly do, pal. You write it?

DEAN

(*Inclining his head to one side modestly*)

How did you guess? 'Er, well, that is, not exactly. I mean, I strung the words together. I don't know who the original author was. Do you?

MORBID INTEREST

Well, might have been me, pal. Course, I can't really say for sure, being the author of so much which has been plagiarized. I've given up trying to keep track of it all.

DEAN

That's a shame. You should really protect your works, you know.

MORBID INTEREST

I suppose so, but that would be a mammoth task. It would take a corps larger than the press corps and the advertising corps, the CIA and the state department put together.

DEAN

But don't you think, the employment picture being what it is, such a corps could be created by executive order and set into action?

NEWSPAPER

(*Peeking out from between* MORBID INTEREST's *fingers*)

Industry rolling again but many remain off work.

MORBID INTEREST

Well, maybe. But wouldn't that sort of take the fun out of it?

DEAN

Hmm. Yes, I suppose it might.

MORBID INTEREST

This way, my own authorship provides the fertilizer for the crop of joy I reap.

DEAN

You reap joy? Oh, Mister Morbid Interest, you are a caution!

MORBID INTEREST

Shh. Not so loud. Sure, I reap joy. I reap tisk-tisk joy with joy, but don't ever tell.

DEAN

Don't worry, I won't. If I told, the jig would be up.

MORBID INTEREST

Mmm, well, not exactly. Telling couldn't do me any harm. It would only harm you, pal. I say, don't ever tell because I like you. You're part of the fun. And if you told, you'd be done.

DEAN

Done?

MORBID INTEREST

Sure. In the first place, nobody would believe you. They'd call it a fiction and fictions are untrue, aren't they?

DEAN
(*Slightly indignant*)

Certainly. Factual objectivity, that's the thing. Fiction is untrue. I guess.

MORBID INTEREST

So, you'd be put away and then I'd have to get along without you. That would mean a drastic shakeup in the organization as it now exists.

DEAN

How does it now exist?

MORBID INTEREST

This way. (*Holds up newspaper and points to headlines*)

NEWSPAPER

Woman found murdered. Police search for maniac responsible.

DEAN

I don't understand.

DEAN DEAN
(*Unable to contain himself longer*)

That, Buster, is journalistic objectivity. We are proclaiming the news. That a woman was murdered is news.

MORBID INTEREST

A young woman, a lovely young woman. Raped and murdered. Bloody doings. Hatchet in skull. Tisk tisk, what fun.

DEAN DEAN

You, sir, are a villain.

MORBID INTEREST

Yes, yes, I are a villain. I stayed up reading because I couldn't sleep. I went in through a cellar door and murdered and raped. I peeked in through the cellar window and saw—raped and murdered. I came with my notebook to see and investigate the circumstances. I inspected a corpse to determine the cause

of death. I demanded to know what had happened. I told myself what had happened. I are a horrible villain. Tee hee.

DEAN

You did all these things?

DEAN DEAN

Don't listen to him. He's trying to obscure good taste and
judgment. He did nothing—

MORBID INTEREST

All those things and more.

DEAN DEAN

—nothing except soak up the smut connected with it, like a
sponge soaking up urine.

MORBID INTEREST

And squeezed the sponge in your face and made you think it
was the finest wine.

NEWSPAPER

Only union men can serve brew.

DEAN

Tell me, Buster, are you a soaker-upper or a squeezer-outer?

MORBID INTEREST

Both, pal. I sow and reap, soak and squeeze. That's what makes
it nice.

DEAN

I see.

DEAN DEAN

Don't be taken in by that rot. He's a simple-minded, smut-
soaked jackass.

MEAN DEAN
(*Popping up from behind the bar*)
Yeah. And so am I.

MORBID INTEREST
Hello, friend. Where have you been?

MEAN DEAN MEAN
(*Peeking up from under the brass rail*)
Hiding in my tingling tissues, tingling to the tissues of it.

MORBID INTEREST
Yes, yes. Grand, wasn't it.

DEAN DEAN
Quiet, you maniacs! Enough of this madness!

MEAN DEAN MEAN
Never enough. We're always thirsty.

MEAN DEAN
And tricky.

MORBID INTEREST
Tricky enough to make you think it's wine. Tee hee.

MEAN DEAN MEAN
Wine to intoxicate you.

MEAN DEAN
Delicious wine you can't resist.

MORBID INTEREST
You should know that, pal. Please be advised.

NEWSPAPER
Only union men can serve brew.

DEAN

Now see here, all I wanted to know was if you found the story interesting. I knew you would and you said you did, so there's no need for all this argument.

DEAN DEAN

But his implications! Can they be excused, dismissed, forgotten?

DEAN

To hell with his implications. I don't know whether there's anything to them or not, so why bother with them.

MEAN DEAN MEAN

You know, all right. You just won't admit it.

DEAN

I *don't* know.

DEAN DEAN

You do know—absolutely and beyond the shadow of a doubt —that right and decency are not to be scoffed at or obscured by the likes of him.

NEWSPAPER

Good motivation needed to absorb extra energy.

MEAN DEAN

The likes of whom?

DEAN DEAN

You, you cad, you.

MEAN DEAN MEAN

Whom?

DEAN DEAN

And you.

MEAN DEAN MEAN, MEAN DEAN, and MORBID INTEREST
(*In unison*)

Whom? Us?

DEAN DEAN

Yes, you. The lot of you.

EUE DEAN
(*Mincingly, from behind bottles on the top shelf*)

Yes, you.

EUE DEAN EUE
(*Astride the handle of a beer tap, waving
his arms and legs*)

You-hoo! I see you. I caught you winking, cutie pie.

SEEDY YOUNG LADY
(*From booth along the wall*)

Tee hee. Oh you!

MORBID INTEREST

Now, pal, I'll prove it to you. Or, rather, you'll prove it to
yourself. Here, between us, is a lovely young hag with hot
pants. Her teeth are rotten, she's posing as twenty but she's
really forty, she's bowlegged, bony-hipped, scaly, hairy, wears
falsies and has bad breath. But, since she winked, you're
madly in love, aren't you.

EUE DEAN EUE

Absolutely. Madly. Quick, let's nibble at that lovely morsel.
Avast! Let's be gone to find a bed.

NEWSPAPER

Dear Martha Right: My boyfriend insisted that if I loved him I should prove it. I do love him and so I proved it. When we first met, he told me he liked me very much and paid a lot of attention to me and flattered me and all.

GHOST OF SHAKESPEARE'S GHOSTS

But virtue, as it never will be mov'd,
Though lewdness court it in a shape of heaven,
So lust, though to a radiant angel link'd,
Will sate itself in a celestial bed,
And prey on garbage.

MORBID INTEREST

You wonder, do you not, how it would be with her?

DEAN

Ugh! It's all the same.

DEAN DEAN

No, not with her. There is such a thing as comeliness, a relative of orderliness. She is an emaciated creature and—

MEAN DEAN MEAN

And later we can toss the prophylaxied corpse into the river.

MEAN DEAN

Who'd miss it?

MORBID INTEREST

Peekaboo, I see you, hiding behind your orderliness.

NEWSPAPER

But later, I noticed a change in him. He just crabbed at me and told me my clothes weren't right.

GHOST

Murder most foul, as in the best it is;
But this most foul, strange, and unnatural.

SEEDY YOUNG LADY

But before we do, I'll insist on one thing—that you treat me like a beauty queen, because I'm bowlegged, bony-hipped, scaly, hairy, wear falsies and spew bad breath.

EUE DEAN EUE

Oh lovely maiden, the sight of you fills me with rapture and sends my yearning soaring like a rocket toward uncharted heavens.

EUE DEAN

Like a rocket heading straight for you-know-what. Tee hee.

MEAN DEAN

Like a rocket with a warhead of pleasurable nuclear derangement.

MEAN DEAN MEAN

Then we'll toss the corpse into the river. Plop-splash, it will go.

SEEDY YOUNG LADY

Well, what are we waiting for? You saw me wink. I know you did. Why don't you saunter over and ask me if I'm the same charming young lady who is the receptionist at Morphine's Departmentalized? I'm not, but I'll say I am.

EUE DEAN EUE

Yes, yes. Stroll, saunter, straunner! Quick, let's get on with the countdown!

MORBID INTEREST

Well?

DEAN DEAN

Never!

DEAN

Now just a damn minute here. Never say never.

EUE DEAN

Attaboy.

DEAN DEAN

She's a hag and I'll have no parts of her. I demand beauty, symmetrical conformation, orderliness.

MORBID INTEREST

So do I, pal, and *from* beauty, and the rest, we both demand the same—in different forms, of course.

DEAN

Ouch! There's the rub.

EUE DEAN

Stop this and concentrate on the bushy bird in the bush.

DEAN DEAN

Buy another beer. Another beer will gain orderliness. Ignore her and drink up.

EUE DEAN EUE

More beer? Never! A whore for the night. She winks—she drinks and thinks and winks.

DEAN DEAN
(*Poking his scowling face out of*
DEAN's *trouser pocket*)

Five dollars, that's all there is. You fool, you hotel-dined, Reet-slapped fool!

NEWSPAPER

But I love him and want to marry him anyway, so I went right on going with him. Then he went to another town one night and stood me up and the next thing I knew, he was marrying this other girl from that other town. Can you help me?

GHOST

whose effect
Holds such an enmity with blood of man
That swift as quicksilver it courses through
The natural gates and alleys of the body,
And with a sudden vigour it doth posset
And curd, like eager droppings into milk,
The thin and wholesome blood; so did it mine. . . .

EUE DEAN

Five bucks, you say?

EUE DEAN EUE

Five rides.

MEAN DEAN

Five stabs.

MEAN DEAN MEAN

Five corpses to toss in the river.

NEWSPAPER

Should doctors be sued for malpractice?

MORBID INTEREST

Go go go, little tweedy.

DEAN DEAN

I'm not finished. Kindly hold your tongues, the lot of you. Now, I would like to point out that the juice which should have gone to her, Sweet Reet, as you insist upon calling her, now coagulates and backs up to form future prostate problems.

MEAN DEAN

That bitch! That cock-teasing bitch!

DEAN DEAN

To whom, sir, do you refer?

MEAN DEAN

To unreamed Reet is whom. Whom else?

MORBID INTEREST

Peekaboo, I see you, prostate problems.

DEAN DEAN

And coagulated, it stagnates.

MEAN DEAN

Well now, that's different.

EUE DEAN

Hey, gang! Hold everything, I think he's on our side!

MEAN DEAN, EUE DEAN EUE, MEAN DEAN
MEAN, and EUE DEAN (*Loudly and together*)

Hip hip hurrah! Hip hip, hurrah!

DEAN DEAN
(*Wryly, after a moment of silence*)

I wish I could say I'm flattered by your cheers, but since they stem from a rash and false assumption, I cannot. Please permit me to continue.

DEAN

So go ahead, continue.

DEAN DEAN

Thank you. Now, this certain young lady of pleasing conformation, eh, bra-lessly delicious, as a matter of fact, has so garnered the organization's collective interest as to preclude a sane decision in this matter of the moment, namely the Seedy Young Lady with bad teeth, bad breath, bad breasts, bad everything.

EUE DEAN EUE
(Sighing rapturously)
Ah, Sweet Reet, how I love, cherish, and adore you.

MEAN DEAN MEAN

Oh, hellish Helwig, I love you with blood and semen boiling, mixing, bubbling.

MEAN DEAN

So much, Sweet Hellishwig, I should have backhanded you and thrown your ass on the couch long ago.

DEAN

He has a point. Had I played the game by those rules, in that context, I would now perchance be embedded in Sweet Reet, like roots in the earth, her whisky, juice, and running sap my nourishment; free of charge I'd be. Instead, I'm brought to this—sopping beer with screaming idiots and leering at a bony hag. Beer-soaked and poorer in every way.

EUE DEAN

(Touched by the pity of it all, wailing a lament in cadence)
Ah, Sweet Reet,
To think it's come to this:
That you are there and I am here,
But for that fiber of desire, disconnected;
That fiber that is stretched so dangerously,
While you—obeying your instructions—
Forbid the contraction which would bring us to each other.

DEAN DEAN

This, you bunch of mushy-minded idiots, is precisely that which I intend you realize. She, I despise; her limbs and torso and vortex, I desire too much. Desire? No. Demand! I, eh, we must have her or be rendered useless by this crazy fixation. And certainly it is nothing but a fixation—unreasonable, unable to be dismissed. What I do not understand is why, in the name of infinite orderliness, should there be this madness to mate madness. Why must I crave the lovely form and motion of her and despise the reflection of us in her, the babbling of the company policy you fools dish up to support a bargaining point? And it is a bargaining point, because if my less for her more succeeds, I'll have my fill of filling her and be gone from her in less than a month, satisfied. But I cannot allow her hold-off to suppress me, nor repress me, or she will end up my master. This would be incongruous. But, by using her hold-off, she plans to get more of me for less of her, like a downtown merchant on a closing-out-sale make, haggling with a sucker over the price. By this offense, she defends herself, offends my manhood, and casts me into the company of screaming idiots leering at a Seedy Young Lady.

DEAN

Sweet Reet, you'll not get me. The bait is the loveliest but I won't be your fish. I see the hook. We're delightfully suited physically, but otherwise we are strangers, as foreign to each other as we would be speaking different languages.

EUE DEAN EUE
(*Close to Dean's ear*)

Psst! She winks. Again.

DEAN

Who?

EUE DEAN EUE

That tender morsel in the booth.

DEAN

That hag?

MEAN DEAN MEAN

That squirming corpse?

DEAN DEAN

Haven't we been through all this? Why must this madness, too, perpetuate itself. Stop, damn it. She's nothing but trouble and our collective desire is not for her.

THE BAR

Pardon me, gentlemen, but I couldn't help overhearing your comments concerning one of my most faithful parishioners, and I find myself compelled to intercede on her behalf.

DEAN

Intercede? How in the name of all that is real and civilized can you intercede?

THE BAR

By being, of course. By being, I intercede quite constantly. That is, I plead the cases of my most faithful by being to them as well as to such heretics as you.

DEAN

Heretic! Me?

THE BAR

Quite. You come and profess a thirst, but it's a shallow thirst, unworthy of my bounteous liquid blessings and not what you pretend it is. Oh there are many such as you. But I know them for the heretics they are the moment I feel their taut bodies touch me. They do not bring with them the need for my support, the spongy thirst of the true believer. No, the true believer leans on me. He does not, as you do, lean against me, or hold himself up using me as a prop. For instance, behold the greedy Seedy Young Lady, who from time to time has captured your attention. Note her attitude of posture.

DEAN

Yes, so ramrod straight it's obvious she's slumping, soggy, shrunken; drinking, groggy, drunken.

THE BAR

You needn't sound so pompous, young fellow. After all, do you consider yourself capable of such devotion? Such faith, such divinity?

NEWSPAPER

"Jazz Mass" packs church.

DEAN

Absolutely not. I have no faith.

THE BAR

And why not?

DEAN

Exactly. Why because why because why because why. That chain reaction from eternity to infinity.

THE BAR

Come come. You must believe in something.

EUE DEAN EUE

Sweet Reet—eue yes! Sweet, unreachable Reet.

MEAN DEAN

The reach for Reet—uncontrolled, unquenched, unquench-able, perpetually stretchable.

DEAN

No, nothing. Unless it's my own ignorance.

SEEDY YOUNG LADY

Hey, honey, it's getting late. All you have to do, sugar, is treat me like a lady and pay me a little tribute, like, say, five dollars worth of drinks. In some other bar.

MORBID INTEREST

Go go go, little tweedy.

EUE DEAN

Yeah, man; go, man.

EUE DEAN EUE

Quickly, too. After all, a bird in the hand . . .

MEAN DEAN

A corpse in the river . . .

SEEDY YOUNG LADY

Look, lambie pie, I'm going to give you one more high sign, and if that don't fetch you, I'll consider you unfetched and I'll go home with that large primate to your right on my arm. But, gee whiz, lover, I wish you'd acknowledge because that slob ain't no fun.

EUE DEAN EUE

Behold the chinful primate:
A large statistic, he;
A tangled web of ho and haw,
A barrel of tee and hee.

DEAN

Mmm, five bucks. I should have known it would be a deal like that.

DEAN DEAN

Think how much draft beer five dollars will buy.

MEAN DEAN
(*Snidely*)

Five barrels of suds!

MEAN DEAN MEAN

To oil the fire.

EUE DEAN

Increase the flame.

EUE DEAN EUE

Shrivel my timbers.

DEAN

Yes.

MEAN DEAN, EUE DEAN, MEAN DEAN MEAN,
and EUE DEAN EUE (*In one loud yell*)

A thousand times *no!*

MEAN DEAN

We will not answer for any crimes which result, master. We'll plead the fifth amendment. Unless you show, here and now, your faith in the Democratic Process and heed our call, the cry of the masses, and give her to us. If you usurp all our rights and douse us with that vile, gas-producing tranquilizer, we'll not answer for the consequences.

EUE DEAN

Beware, Mister President, a revolution threatens if you so much as touch that five spot while in the vicinity of this Temple of T.

EUE DEAN EUE

Yes, a revolution. And now she winks. See? See, there she winks again. Twice! Two winks so you'll know what she means, directly at you, master, so there can be no mistake. Let's go.

MEAN DEAN MEAN

Away, away! Avast! Up anchor! My sword is ready; my blood boils for the delight of attack.

DEAN

Quiet, you cads, or it will be solitary confinement for the lot of you.

DEAN DEAN
(Aside, to himself)

At last, some sense. Some leadership, a guiding light.

MEAN DEAN

Solitary confinement! Ha! And the keeper our prisoner. Just try that solitary confinement, master, just try it and see how lonesome you'll be.

THE BAR

Ah hem! Gentlemen, you are off on a useless tangent. It's what I've been trying to tell you—you pursue that path in vain. You can go telescoping and falling into yourself for ever and ever Amen. You telescope endlessly and you fall into a bottomless pit. You can't imagine the folly of it. In fact, you can imagine very little when you get right down to cases, you heretics. So, in the name of all that is sacred and correct, lean on me and stop your incessant babble. Preserve sanctity: an eye for an eye and a beer for a dime.

EUE DEAN

A whore for the night.

MEAN DEAN

A cadaver to slice.

DEAN

Five bucks.

EUE DEAN EUE

Five rides.

MEAN DEAN MEAN

Five executions.

EUE DEAN EUE

Ashes to ashes and butts to butts, if she don't get five, I'll go nuts!

THE BAR

Hush! Sinners all! Your vile thoughts are an outrage to this blessed house.

MEAN DEAN

A self-perpetuating outrage.

THE BAR

Repent, and suffer your money to come unto me, for I am the kingdom of booze and the glory and power of oblivion.

DEAN

For five bucks.

MEAN DEAN
(*Bitterly*)

Five barrels of suds. Ugh!

EUE DEAN EUE
(*Shrieking*)

No suds! Five rides for five.

MEAN DEAN MEAN

Yes, or dadblast it, I'll blow the whole show to hell.

DEAN

To where?

EUE DEAN

To the door with a wink and a nod. Quick!

MEAN DEAN

Or I'll take this stool and heave it into that mirror.

THE BAR

Such willful destruction is a sin, and if you persist, you'll be ostracized.

DEAN

Don't be so touchy, your reverence. Really, the boys mean no harm.

MEAN DEAN
(*Caustically*)

Just speaking up for our rights, governor. Our inalienable rights.

EUE DEAN

That's right—inalienable. That, at least.

EUE DEAN EUE

The Fair Maiden rises, like spring mist from a shallow bog, casts us another look—long and carefully—picks up her pocketbook, turns and—hark hark—sashays to the portal. Avast! Up anchor!

EUE DEAN

Yes, quick, avast! Down that glass of suds and let's be going.

DEAN
(*After watching closely as the* SEEDY YOUNG LADY
hip-sways and slow-whips past him, close to him in

the narrow aisle, leaving in her wake a symphony of
scents—sweat, blood, and salty desire)
No, she's a hag. Worse. I can't take it. We're not going.

MEAN DEAN MEAN
(Climbing to the top of a stool)
Maniacs unite! Solidarity will win our cause! Heed this call
to glory! March on the filthy capitalist pig!

MEAN DEAN, EUE DEAN, and EUE DEAN EUE
(Aroused—if not to march, at least to profanity)
Jesus Christ! Shakespeare! Freud! Marx!

EUE DEAN
(Breathlessly, whispering)
She's going . . .

EUE DEAN EUE
Through the door . . .

MEAN DEAN
Quick, master, she expects you to follow.

DEAN
I won't. She's a hag.

EUE DEAN EUE
(Rolling on the floor, retching with uncontrollable sobs
and moans)
Oh master, a hag, but a hag through which beauty may
flooow . . .

MEAN DEAN
(With a vindictive sneer)
Too late!

MEAN DEAN MEAN
(*Sliding down off his perch*)
You wouldn't listen to me and now it's too late. She's gone, oh mighty master, gone!

EUE DEAN EUE
(*With a wretched sob*)
Gone . . .

MORBID INTEREST
(*After a moment of complete silence*)
Tee hee. Ha ha ha. Haw! Peekaboo!

THE BAR
Now now! None of that giggling. Retribution is mine. Order up.

DEAN
Okay. Give me one more. This time, give me a shot on the side. Make it a double. Then I'm going home. Enough of these dramatics.

THE BAR
Such a small capacity for faith.

DEAN
No capacity at all.

EUE DEAN
(*Still sobbing*)
You shouldn't have let her get away. That was too much. I can't stand much more. Do you hear? I can't stand much more.

DEAN

You'll stand it, all right. As long as I'm the boss, you'll stand it all.

MEAN DEAN

Just wait until elections roll around, Mister President. We'll fix your wagon.

MEAN DEAN MEAN

Yes, just wait and see, Mister President. After the ballots have been counted . . .

DEAN

Quiet. We're going home.

EUE DEAN

The ultimate tragedy.

MEAN DEAN

(*Nudging the others, pointing up the aisle*)

Oh no, not quite ultimate. Look. Here comes a pageant Mister President should watch closely. Ah yes, doom hangs thick in the air, tobacco scented.

(*Down the aisle come* PALLBEARERS *carrying an opened casket. They stop in front of* DEAN *and wait patiently while grave diggers chop through the barroom floor and dig a hole. Then they lift the casket again, extend it over the hole, and pause a moment for* DEAN *to see.* DEAN *peeks and sees the premier. Then the* PALLBEARERS *lower the casket holeward, chanting to the tune of "Bringing In the Sheaves"*)

PALLBEARERS

Getting more for less
Getting more for less
. We are get-ting

Mo-ore
Getting mo-ore
For less.

(*Then the* PALLBEARERS *throw their gloves into the grave and walk away slowly toward the thick, hanging doom smoke*)

An Ice Cube in A Frying Pan

I KNOW
SHE IS

there's this large door glass fancy and
classy and she's in there in there know
she's in there hack at it hacking and hacking with splinters flying past ears through
hair and doorman ugly doorman with
dirty boots standing on the nice clean
carpet but there she is standing in the
middle of the floor with her mouth wide
open and her eyes wide open is she smil-

ALWAYS
A DOORMAN

ing or what or is it shock or what happened here anyhow and the the doorman
is coming with a hatchet swinging trying
to duck quick get away chase the girl
the lovely girl all over the rug in bare
feet running and running and feeling the
tickle but the doorman keeps coming

TAKE OFF
YOUR BOOTS

with the hatchet and she's laughing and
running away then standing and looking
and buzzing silently sexuating but she's
laughing too and running and duck watch
out for that damn doorman with that
damn hatchet he's coming and she's running away running all over the place in

145

her bare feet must catch her must must have her duck here comes that doorman again trying to sink that hatchet oh lord that would be the end look out duck get that thing can't get her without that hatchet because she's running all over the rug in her bare feet laughing duck he's big and tough and that hatchet duck he's got the arm holding the arms caught then out then caught again must get out and get that hatchet ah caught it by the handle now chase that damn doorman

GO GO GO out of here out out you foul smelling cur
LITTLE TWEEDY you beast go on out and read the paper find out all about it in the paper after it's been done after it all happened when it's too late to do anything about it go on out and leave us but she's still laughing and running ah ha but with this hatchet she'll not get far she'll get caught and yes yes she's wearing a fur coat and she's nude underneath she's showing it off oh lord she's nice she can't get far can't get out of the room she can run all she wants to now but she can't get away she'll soon

OH PLEASE tire and fall and the rug is so ticklish and
IT WON'T HURT thick and nice and everything is nice now with that damn doorman gone except for the music that jazz from a psych ward someplace sounds out of this world musicians beating pots and pans all over the room like stereo and she's running again in time to the music dancing on the run but she'll fall soon and she'll be had yes

ONE WAY yes she's falling and being tackled by her
OR ANOTHER lovely ankles and calves and thighs but

that fur coat it won't open and she won't open her legs she's laughing still laughing with her eyes and mouth wide open as if she can't breath but she can because she's laughing and keeping it to herself and finding how to get that fur coat off is tough but she's down now oh squirming and wriggling but down so it's nice squirm some more ah ha yes yes right through the fur coat with her legs so tight together but the hatchet will fix that yes the hatchet will loosen her up in it goes and now she won't squirm as much just enough and she'll relax yes yes ah ha relax with her mouth wide open and her eyes wide open and now the fur coat opens and her legs open and

He awoke, sat up, and felt the throb and gush, then felt the letdown and a vague disquieting guilt, a mingling of guilt and disappointment.

Nothing to do now.

Nothing?

Unless I am being turned into a raving maniac by my stupid fixation for that empty-headed she next door, an abundance of seed and need.

Empty-headed? Recall, my seedy needy friend, her frenzied breaths and moans, her dilemma. Do you suppose that expression of internal chaos is the result of empty-headedness? If it were completely empty, her head, you from her would now protrude. No, not empty-headed. And what dreams do you suppose kept her up while you stomped the brass rail? What dreams do her true energies drive through her? And what, except walls and cowardice, inundated conscience and crippled will, perpetuates this misdirected and wasteful discharge of energy?

What? And so what?

I'll tell you what, my friend: the big irony, denied but lurking like her desire, always laughing, laughing like an audience of uncouth brainwashed oafs at the modest maiden found naked and trying to hide herself behind the inadequate shields of hands and arms, bent over, thighs tight together.

You confuse me, Ally, with your big irony and tight thighs. And I do not wish to be confused. I wish to decide once and for all either to have her one way or another, or to be rid of my damning urge for her one way or another. I want no more hatchet-swinging dreams and miscarried discharges. I want no more dillydallying with her, listening to her stupid, miserable tearful tirades and prayers. I want to have my fill of her fill of me and then be up and gone and my undistracted self again. And, unless I deceive myself, she would, if nicely handled, be as much in favor of this arrangement as I, if for different reasons. In other words, she's asking for it.

More or less, yes. She's asking tat for tit, more or less. Remember?

Could I forget? But she won't get it.

Oh no? Are you so sure?

She can't. Impossible. A mismatch.

Certainly a mismatch, but she's winning. Remember how she cried in your ear, prayed in your ear?

Hush! I suppose she is winning, although the lack of formal rules in this game makes scoring difficult.

Difficult or not, consider the hatchet-swinging dream and deny, if you will, that she had much to do with putting it in your sleeping hand.

Not she alone.

To be sure, but she is the one necessary ingredient in the concoction. Admit that much.

All right, yes, I guess she is. But I'll fix that.

You should have fixed that hours ago.

When I came home—
You remember?
She was waiting—
And?
When I tried—
Pitter patter . . . ?
Yes, but I followed.
And how you did, hero.
Followed her in—
Blind drunk you were, hero.
And—
And she prayed.
Dear Lord, she said—
Make him understand.
Oh God, she said—
Help me.
Eue Dean, she moaned—
Please!
And there she lay—
In a ball on the floor.
Clutching her knees—
Praying.
Praying?
Saying, Dear Lord, Oh God, help me.
Yes, yes, I remember now. Remember it all.
Plainly. It was . . . .
Horrible?
Not exactly.
Wonderful?
No, certainly not that.
Terrible?
Partly.
Saying, Dear Lord, Oh God, help me.
Saying, Dean get away. Dean you're drunk,
Dean stop.

Crying.

Again crying.

And yet—

Yes, following.

Following you out, to the living room, to the kitchen, to the coffee she had made for you, drunken Dean.

Eue Dean, she said.

Can't I understand, she said.

Don't you see, she said.

The decent thing, she said.

And yet—

Yes, following.

To the door.

On the other side of the golden V-shaped knocker.

Pleading.

For what?

Who knows?

Saying, Dear Lord, Oh God, help me.

Clutching you.

Holding me.

Stopping you.

But I—

Rippingly—

Left, torn shirt and all.

And now?

Yes, still.

So, Ally, hero, my friend, you are, I feel sure, ripe for the prowl. The fire escape awaits.

Oh no, not that. Turn myself into a prowler? Sneak along the fire escape, peep in her window, scratch like a pup begging for admittance? No!

But she's on the brink of.

All she needs is a little push, true.

Haven't you been pushing, more than a little?

Hmm. Yes, but—

And for how long?

All right, I'll forget her. I'll call Sandra tomorrow, first thing.

Bluffer.

Sandra is lovely, prettier than Rita; that is, not as sexy, stagy, show-off-ish. Sandra is relaxing, a listener, almost my kind.

Think, hero, of all the Sandras in the world peering at you with attentive ears and pleading eyes and running soft hands through your hair, laughing and loving. Then think of one Sweet Reet, trucking, helwig wiggling through the midst of all that and—

Dear Lord, Oh God, help me.

And tell yourself how all the Sandras would ease the barb of one Reet left untasted.

Opportunity, you say?

Certainly. You are out on the fire escape. It's a hot night. Can't sleep. You wake her, carefully, make her look out her window and find you there on the fire escape.

Suppose she thinks I'm a prowler?

You speak softly to her immediately, calm her fears, guide her attention to you, sleepless. She will be drowsy, bed-warm, close to the elemental and far from frills.

Well, I could wake her, somehow.

It could be done.

But—

Faint heart never . . .

I don't wish to win her, I wish to have her.

There's a difference?

In duration.

But initially it's the same.

All right, all right.

After all, it must be resolved one way or another.

Then let's resolve it one way, not another. Attaboy. No substitutes.

For her? For her, that wiggling Helwig, that jitterbugging juxtaposition of morality over moist lust, for her there can be no substitute.

The lust is yours, the moisture hers.

If mine alone, then by its sheer intensity I'll burn it into her and make it hers, too.

It will go: Hisssssssssst.

His compulsion's momentum raised him up and out of bed. He slipped into trousers and went through the darkened apartment to the living-room window. He removed the screen quietly and stepped over the sill onto the fire escape. He went, feeling like a salmon swimming upstream, driving through much fear and difficulty, powered by more desire.

Outside it was a warm night, warmer than he had thought. He felt naked against the building's stone wall, looking down at the street lights and neon signs.

OPEN ALL NIGHT

But he thought of her and how she must be, asleep, abed, a lax and dewy nest to ease the ferocious knot of tight anticipation and longing inside him, and he shuffled along the rusting strips of grating, past the door to the hall, toward her window. The beep of a car horn startled him as he leaned toward her window. His pulse throbbed in his temples and his heart beat at its cage. His bare feet slid an inch closer, his fingers made contact with the outside frame of her window, his eyes scanned the blinking neon below.

IF IT'S NEW
BUICK HAS IT

OPEN ALL NIGHT
MORROW'S MOTEL   VACANCY

OPEN ALL NIGHT
SATISFACTION WHILE U WAIT

Then a contraction of fear yanked him back and he froze. He fought an urge to glide quickly over the rusty grating back to his living-room window and inside to the safety of privacy. Out here, over the blinking neons amid the hum of wee-hour traffic between moments of haunted silence and footsteps of unknown persons on the concrete sidewalk he felt like a hunted animal, like a fugitive cornered and doomed, with a thousand pursuers bearing down on him, ready to tear him apart limb from limb. But he turned his face to the building and that helped, and in a moment he pulled his mind away from fear and back to her. Then he continued toward her window, easing his fingers back to her window frame, creeping along the grating, finally within peeking distance. He craned his neck around the corner of her window and looked in.

A luminous blank sheet accosted his eyes and he withdrew his head quickly and quickly considered retreating back to the safety of his own apartment because, he snapped at himself, something had gone wrong. Then he reacted to that consideration by reasoning that the blank sheet was her window shade and the brightness of it came from a light inside. He peeled himself from the wall and poked his head around the corner of her window frame again. His eye traveled to a spot at the lower corner of the shaded window where a shaft of light emerged from a hole, and the rest of him followed his eye. He stooped and peeked in through the hole in the shade. He leaned his peeking eye close to the screen that came between himself and her holey shade and more of the room came into view. By moving his head up and down and from side to side he soon located his object. She was prone on her bed, reading, head propped up on a pillow. Visible to him at this moment were her profile, pincurled hair, arm, shoulder and back, arching down from high-propped shoulders to waist, unseen below the surface of mattress. Up from the bottom hung one lower leg and foot, carrying on a pantomime of flexing and unflexing. Otherwise, she remained motionless. So did he. He waited. He wasn't sure why or what he expected her to do, but he waited.

She rubbed her nose before turning a page, then tilted her head to a new angle to read from the top of the left page. As he became accustomed to his new station, he felt the cool night air on his bare back and shivered intermittently. But he wasn't sure which caused the spasmodic shivers—the air on his back or his awkward waiting way station, his post close to a way to her.

But such a way. For shame!

A way anyway.

He might, he speculated, attract her attention. A cough during a lull between the hum of cars would be enough. But how would she react to that? Maybe it would be better to call to her softly but loud enough to let her know it was he and not a stranger. Still, her reaction to that approach was uncertain. She might explode into a violent scream of fear. For instance, what book was she reading? A story of love, possibly one critics called earthy, warm, sympathetic? Fine. Or, for all he knew, it might be a nonfiction book, transporting her from her mundane paradox to a mundane paradox redecorated. But suppose she were reading a murder mystery, or one of those terrifying science-fiction tales of lusty horror from another world? In that case, how would she react to lusty him from another apartment? Any peep out of peeking Dean, he decided, might result in an operatic climax. So, even calling her name would be taking a risk.

Risk?

Risk what?

Yes, I see. At the first fresh, glistening high C out of her, I homeward bound would be.

Two leaps worth. That's a risk?

He chuckled to himself thinking how he might call her name then run, then listen to her tomorrow as she recounted how she had heard her name called in the middle of the all-asleep night.

And why doesn't she sleep?

Two guesses.

Me and who else?

Thee and she and the mystery.

Hmm. It would be so much simpler if she would only sleep. Then it would be slow, cautious, certain, with an element of the artistic.

Then, suddenly, he was startled by Rita's sudden jounce to a sit to a stand to a walk—across the room to a dresser, pink-and-whitely, bare topped, like a pink and white island girl with skin creased from weighted contact with creased sheets, with complete self-absorption, oblivious to flouncy mammilla and outlandish, curled hair tight to her head.

Mean Dean winced. He tightened his hold on her window's outside frame and pressed his nose against their separation, her shaded screen. And took a deep breath, the kind of deep breath that follows a sudden change of air.

Whowee!

Whoweedeedee!

In action!

Such action!

Such plural action!

Such plural, unsupplemented action!

The object of her trip, he learned, was a cigarette. She put a match to it while standing in front of the dresser mirror, then picked up an ashtray, and returned to bed and book. This time she sat crosslegged with her back to the headboard and her book in her lap, reading and smoking.

I could, in one swift lunge, rip through this separating screen as if it were an antiquated Shalt-Not, flip the switch on her bedside lamp, and replace both book and cigarette. This old shaded screen would give easily. I'd be inside and on my way to the light in no time. She'd see it was me and find her scream choked by the short history of us. The boldness of the action might overwhelm her and render her a crippled tit-for-tat player, and I might assume the command her book now exerts over her senses. I might assume all command of her and her senses. She would have no bedroom to run to because she would be in her bedroom. Anyway, she would be too surprised to run, too surprised to do anything. I would command. I would have her on my terms.

Tut tut, my friend, you should know by now that soaring enthusiasm must be kept chained to an immovable ball and chain of doubt. Otherwise, you sin against reason.

For such a sin I will go to hell?

Not for the sin against doubt, not according to the scriptures, not that hell. But you will nevertheless go to your own jolly old hell on earth, because your tentative plan is built on suppositions and suppositions fold under the ragged ends of doubt; but the ragged ends, folded under, remain. And turn up later.

To hell with your ragged ends, Ally, and as for jolly, I'm for that. Maybe that's my trouble—I've not yet created my own jolly old hell on earth, being unduly concerned with the ragged edges of doubts. I'm a sinner against the church, bound for that mythical furnace. In order to save myself from that furnace, I should break the chain of doubt and have faith—faith in the Dear Lord, faith in the Economy, faith in Freedom, faith in Motherhood, faith in the President and faith that the courts of the land are in fact dispensers of a justice which coincides with Higher Justice, whatever it is.

Your foolishness, my friend, threatens our alliance. Certainly one glance from the window of an airplane should convince you that man's sense of justice, for instance, cuts across the grain of Nature's mysterious orderliness, if in fact what we cannot understand is orderly. Recall the absurd patchwork of fields in the country, the crags and crevices of mortar in the city—both authored by that most honorable absurdity which has created and perpetuated the political boundary. Do you suppose man's superimposed finite orderliness over Nature's infinite scheme results in true orderliness?

Perhaps you have a point, Solomon. But, considering my stretched underwear, which way do I turn to find orderliness? Do I ignore my lust because it is surely purely carnal, because I do not want the lady's lifelong company, because I yearn for skin-to-skin, membrane-to-membrane contact with her for sensuous delight and copulation, for intercourse with her physical being only? Or do I superimpose over that pure lust that which I have been taught to use to dilute lust—a conscience? Is my innate lust to be tied to conscience, as you would have me tie enthusiasm to doubt?

The ball and chain of conscience is an acquired contrivance, as open to doubt as your sense of reality. It is not comparable to the ball and chain of doubt. Rather, it is a blind, unbound enthusiasm itself. Doubt presents itself to all who are not blind, but most are. It comes as a storm to ruin homes, as a tidal wave to sweep the conscience-stricken into the sea, as a disease replacing conquered disease. It comes from the unknown and the unknowable and we can trace it no further than the limits of our imaginations. Conscience is the ball and chain of the blind and those who have joined the ranks of the absurd, who march in step, the good church-goers who do not realize the existence of the unknowable they profess to worship. Conscience is to them what doubt is to you, my friend.

You flatter me into submission, Mephistopheles. Now, while I wallow, let's get back to the matter at hand.

Or more precisely, not at hand.

Yes, beyond hand and screen. But advise me so that the matter can become at hand, dear Ally.

Ah ha. I was hoping you would seek my advice. I have a simple remedy: rape her.

Rape her?

Yes, rape her. In the name of the ball and chain of doubt, of the infinite orderliness which now stretches your underwear, of your expressed desire and her denied desire, rape her.

But—

Allow me to explain my position. She is, after all, a simple person, concerned with little more than her physical functions, chained to that feeble and artificial ball and chain, her conscience. And she is also pulled by the desire for that comfort we call marching in step—matrimony, monogamy, or successive polygamy. Her aim, therefore, is your demise, and your aim, her desire. She would feel most out of sorts should she leave the soothing comforts of mass absurdity to attempt to join you in your lonely absurdity. And likewise, we would not be us if we tried to join her in-step absurdity. Besides, all you desire is her participation in that which she desires, but participation unhampered by her silly ball and chain. Hence, by utilizing her acquired delight in violence, we can exert the external force necessary for her to resolve and compromise her dilemma, and do it in such a way as to leave her still smugly tied to her ball and chain. Rape her, nicely nicely.

I say, dear Ally, this raping business could be a bit messy, you know.

Yes, like feeding a hungry lion. But I say rape her nicely nicely, with finesse, if possible.

And suppose, the old ball game being what it is, nicely nicely isn't possible?

Now you're on the right track, my friend. Now you've acknowledged being tied to the ball and chain of doubt.

That doesn't answer the question, Solomon Satyr.

I believe you hung your question on a suppose, did you not?

I did.

Then, just as readily, let us suppose nicely nicely is possible.

Then we're right back to start, Ally, nose to screen, object not in hand.

Not quite. Now, hanging as we are from two suppositions, we are prepared to make a choice, but doubting the correctness of our choice as we make it, therefore prepared for the zig and zag, flexible.

To crash in and nicely nicely rape may result in an undesirable drama, a dropping of the nicely nicely, more drama, also undesirable, and a resolution scene with me cast as villain. On the other hand, to retreat to safety and not attempt the nicely nicely will perpetuate the worship of this grotesque, paralyzing, seed-scattering fixation.

Correct. So, should we pick one supposition to swing from and should we select incorrectly, we will swing to jail—one jail or the other, to the county workhouse or the psychic rothouse.

Yes, and if we retreat to safety we gain nothing. Whereas, if we charge in and nicely nicely, and if nicely nicely works, we eliminate this gnawing infection—

Therefore be it resolved that, with due regard for sound vibrations, sex fixations, and Sweet Reet's rebuffing invitations, we shall, after deciding upon a definite approach, rape Reet, nicely nicely.

Question:

To bring her to thee or thee to her?

If the former:

The separating screen remains intact, unless Sweet Reet sees fit to remove it.

The odds on this removal?

Please, my friend. Such odds are too subject to unforeseen variables to estimate.

Then, if the latter—me to her?

Again, a host of unpredictable variables.

Why so unpredictable?

There ain't no reason. It's the policy.

Oh, well, in that case—

Determination for copulation creating screen-breaking momentum resulting in unscheduled arrival, a certain amount of surprise and an incalculable reaction to this action with which nicely nicely will have to cope, relying on old reliable doubt for flexibility, is how.

Quite so.

So—

Dean's fingers crept up the brick wall to the wooden frame of her window screen and slid along on the layer of grime and dust which covered it, feeling for something to hold onto and pull. He stood to permit his searching fingers a complete investigation. But he found nothing to use to pull out her screen. He paused and again considered calling to her, softly, and when she came, ask entrance, and when she refused, break in. At least that way she'd know he was here and the element of surprise would not be as severe. But the element of surprise, if severe, might work in his favor, he told himself. So, he finally decided to place the palms of his hands against the screen and push; when it gave, leap through the hole into Helwig's wiggling bedroom, hellishly, prepared for the zigzag of unpredictables.

He raised his hands and placed his palms against the screen and was about to press when he heard a sudden clang.

There was a seemingly long moment when he was unable to relate the clang to anything known or supposed. Then, again suddenly, he became aware of something coming toward him from his left. He turned and looked just as it was upon him—a bulk, moving, dark, legged, faced, capped, uniformed. The bulk was upon him now and, suddenly, he saw a bright flash, like lightning, and heard a buzzing drone and saw a night stick. Then, momentarily, he dissolved from total awareness of himself and the descending bulk into a drugged-like state of partial awareness, an underwater echo chamber peopled by demons.

He was next aware of being dragged to his feet by a policeman he didn't know, a beatman. The beatman held a bully-club in his right hand and used it for short, rapid blows to Dean's head and back while using the other hand to haul him to his feet. Then Dean felt himself—still only vaguely aware, still floating on an ethereal wave far away from remembrance —being driven, pushed, pulled, shoved toward the fire-escape door, through it, and into the apartment-house hallway. As the door clanged closed behind them, the beatman was speaking in a loud, husky voice, telling him to move, saying something about going to the station with no shirt unless he wanted to pick one up quickly. He asked Dean where he lived and, since they stood just outside the door to Dean's apartment, Dean pointed. The beatman tried the door and found it locked. His hand left the door knob to be immediately replaced by another hand. The custodian, in bathrobe and slippers, was unlocking the door, saying something about always thinking there was something the matter with that young feller. The beatman shoved Dean inside his apartment and ordered him to find a shirt and jacket and be quick about it. The custodian, when Dean lagged, still stunned, brushed past them and disappeared into Dean's bedroom and emerged with the torn shirt, shoes, and jacket Dean had worn the day before. Then the beatman shoved him out into the hall again, now lined with sleepy faces peering from half-opened doorways, including Rita's pincurled head. She called, "Dean, where are you going? Hey, where are you taking him? Hey, what's going on here?" But nobody answered her. Dean felt himself float-walking down the hall toward the steps to the front door, nudged by the beatman's bullyclub, and heard as if from a great distance the whispered questions from the half-opened doors. Outside they were met by a patrol car and Dean was pushed into the back seat and they were off, moving, whirring over the blacktopped street with the siren screaming, moaning its cry of victory to the early morning. They rounded a corner on squealing tires and screaming siren, then another. Then they pulled up to the rear entrance of number one police station and Dean was pushed out and whisked inside in front of the waving bullyclub.

The bright lights hurt his eyes and, in his torn, unbuttoned shirt, unlaced shoes, jacket over his shoulder, he felt embarrassed, naked, a stranger in a police station he visited often. Up on the platform and behind the desk sat a familiar face—Sergeant Jackson. Dean responded to this one speck of familiarity by moving toward him, mouth drooping, beseeching silently.

"Book him," said the beatman. "Charge him later."

"Him?" Sergeant Jackson's aged face crinkled into incredulousness.

"Yeah, him. Who'd you think? Me?" said the beatman.

"You know who this guy is?"

"No, do you?"

The sergeant shook his head slowly, apparently deciding not to continue the exchange while the beatman was expansive with the pride of capture. He picked up the arrest pad and a pen and asked Dean, "Name?"

Dean stared dumbly.

"What's your name, feller? He wants to know your name," snapped the beatman.

"I know his name," said the sergeant as he scratched it on the pad.

"Address!" ordered the beatman.

"Yeah, where does he live," said the sergeant.

"Apartment sixteen, Charter House, Market Street," said the beatman.

"Hmm," said the sergeant as he wrote.

"Okay, let's move," said the beatman, nudging Dean again. "Upstairs to fingerprinting we go."

Dean felt himself being shoved along again to the door leading to the stairs, through it, up the stairs with the beatman holding him firmly by the upper arm under the armpit.

"Now, feller," said the beatman, as they went through the second floor door and headed toward the door with frosted glass marked *Identification,* "we'll find out who you really are."

Dean sighed a huff of mirth, remembering Mark's words:

Where am I and what am I doing here? Funny. They want to know who they have, and I want to know what has me. Real funny.

Then he found himself on the inside of the door, released by the beatman, who closed the door with a glass-rattling bang. Behind the low desk in the center of the bare hardwood floor sat another familiar face. Dean didn't know his name, only that he was one of the three identification clerks.

"Hey," said the clerk, cheerfully, "what brings you here at this hour?"

Dean found his voice. "He does," he said, pointing to the beatman.

"Him! Hey, what goes?"

The beatman moved toward the clerk, watching Dean as he went, smiling. "Peeping Tom," he said proudly. "With suspicion of intent to assault and ravish. Suspicion of murder and rape, too." He said it as if he were talking about what a nice wife and family he had.

The clerk stood. "What?" He came toward Dean wearing an expression of pained inquiry. "You?"

"Yeah, him!" growled the beatman.

"You were caught peeping, a Peeping Tom?"

"On the fire escape of the place where he lives at," said the beatman. "Feller from another apartment house seen him through his telescope. Called in. I caught him redhanded. Looked like he was just about to bust in, too."

"Where's the chief?" muttered Dean.

"Well I'll be damned," said the clerk.

"Okay," snapped the beatman, "let's go." He pushed Dean and they shuffled off to the far side of the room where the fingerprinting equipment stood in ever-readiness. The clerk followed, mumbling to himself.

Dean's fingers were inked by the clerk while the beatman watched, leaning forward and peering at the procedure with an interest close to avarice. Dean's inked fingers were pressed one at a time onto specified squares blocked out on the identification form on the table. Then the process was repeated with the other hand.

"I want to call a lawyer," said Dean. "Or else Chief Alex. Let me call the chief." The clerk and beatman ignored him.

When the fingerprinting was over, the beatman grabbed Dean under the armpit again and said, by way of a farewell to the clerk, "A nut. A real, live nut."

"Could be our rabbit," said the clerk.

"Darn right he could," said the beatman. "He's going right down to interrogation right now."

"Might have to wait a while. Got quite a lineup down there. Been shoving them through all night."

"Well," said the beatman with a confidential smile to the clerk, "maybe this specimen will get special consideration when they find out how I caught him."

"Yeah," said the clerk, as if that important thought had just occurred to him, too.

"Okay, feller, let's move," commanded the beatman. They moved out and down the stairs again, through the sergeant's domain to a room farthest from the side door and in.

Dean's stomach convulsed with a familiar nausea. Around the room on chairs lining the wall sat suspects—vagrants, a platoon of the sexually forlorn, big and small, well-dressed and ragged, hard-featured and feminine, black and white, jittery and asleep, waiting. They were guarded by two patrolmen with rifles, one at the door Dean entered and another at a far door marked *Interrogation*. Dean recalled the inside of the interrogation room as he sat in the chair nearest the door he had just entered. It had a low stool and a large, overhead light, no windows, a loud wall fan. It smelled of dust and varnish and the hint of sweat and urine.

"Hey," said Dean to anyone who would listen, "I want to call a lawyer."

No one answered. The beatman carried on a whispered discussion with the patrolman guarding the interrogation room door, then gained admittance. The patrolman eyed Dean and they waited.

Finally, after what seemed like a very long time, the beat-man came out and beckoned Dean with a sneering smile and a forefinger.

Dean felt himself leave the chair and follow. He was met in the doorway by three plainclothesmen he did not recognize and a freshly questioned suspect, a Negro with a scarred face wearing work clothes, with saliva trickling down his chin. The Negro stared straight ahead as he went through the door. The dumb-animal expression on his dark, scarred face frightened Dean, and the shock of realization suddenly hit him. He began to tremble.

Then he found himself seated on a low stool under the bright light surrounded by the three plainclothesmen. The *Chronicle* lay on the floor in front of the stool. Dean's eyes caught *BOOM PREDICTED* in the lower left corner, then he forced his gaze back up to the three surrounding faces. They were puffy faces, unfamiliar, yet strangely mundane. He wondered where they had come from and why he didn't know them. He wondered how many other unfamiliar police-men there were in town at the moment working on the murder. They stared at him like a team of scientists at an unknown phenomenon. The wall fan zinged steadily, loudly in his left ear.

After the initial pause and exchange of stares, Dean was asked his name, address, and whether he had a previous criminal record.

"You might as well tell us," said one detective when Dean gave a negative response. "We'll find out anyway."

"But I don't have a record," said Dean.

"Are you sure?"

"Sure I'm sure."

The largest of the three, a man with hanging jowls who looked more like a prosperous businessman than a detective, took up the questioning. The other two remained silently intent listeners.

The questioner asked his age. Dean told him twenty-three. Then his occupation:

"You work?"

"Sure I work."

"Where?"

"The Chronicle," said Dean, pointing to the floor in front of him, to *BOOM PREDICTED*. "I wrote that story."

"Which one?"

"About the murder. And the sidebar about the maniac responsible."

The detective bent over with a deflated moan and picked up the paper, opened it, and inspected it with head tilted.

"That's my name on the one story," said Dean.

"So it is," said the detective. "Well, well, well."

"Now look," said Dean, "I can explain. Or, I think I can. Well, I don't know. You see, this girl next door to me, we've been dating, you know."

"Oh?"

"Yeah. We went out to dinner last night, as a matter of fact."

"Is that so."

"Yeah. Then we had a little, eh, a little difference of opinion over something, you know, nothing really, and, well, I went out and got a little juiced up on beer and, well, I just . . ." He shrugged.

"Tell us more," said the detective.

"Well, I came home and slept awhile, then I thought I'd go see her. You know."

"But you thought you'd use the window instead of the door, just for fun?"

"No, not exactly. I . . ." Dean scratched the front of his sleep-matted crewcut. "I thought I'd sneak over and call her name and have a laugh out of it tomorrow. Today, that is."

"Oh?"

"Yeah."

"Officer Stanley says you were about to push on her screen and break in."

"Well, I had my hands on it, but . . ."

"Yes?"

"Oh hell! I want to see a lawyer."

"I suppose so."

"Look, it. . . . Why don't you go get the girl and ask her?"

"We will, we will. All in good time. First we want to talk to you."

Dean slumped down on the stool and listened to the monotonous fan.

"Anyway," said the detective, "We're out on the fire escape with our hands on the screen. Then what?"

"Then that guy came along and bashed me over the head with his club, that's what." Dean felt his head. A large lump had formed, but although the spot was sore, he could find no trace of blood.

"Just before you were going to bust in on the girl?"

"No. I mean, I. . . ."

"Well?"

Dean shrugged.

"Tell us," said the detective, "what were you thinking about out there on the fire escape with no shirt and no shoes?"

"Thinking about?"

"Yes, thinking about."

"I don't know. I, I, I guess I was just full of beer."

"Beer?"

"Yes."

"Beer makes me sleepy. Makes me sleep soundly, too. How is it that beer got you out there?"

"I don't know. Not beer alone, I guess."

"Ah ha! What else?"

"Well, we've been dating, you see, and . . ."

"Yes, I see."

"No, no. Nothing like that. I mean, she's a nice girl and all that. She wouldn't do anything promiscuous."

"But you would, eh?"

"Well, I wanted to, but—"

"But she wouldn't let you."

"Well, yes, I guess so."

"You guess so?"

"Well, it wasn't as clear-cut as all that."

"How was it?"

"Well, she's looking for a husband, I guess."

"Aren't most girls her age?"

"Yeah, sure, but I'm not the type for her. I mean, she's nice physically and all that, but we just don't. . . ."

"Don't what?"

"Don't go together. I mean, our interests and beliefs and things."

"No, I don't suppose you do."

"No, you don't get what I mean. I'm a newspaper reporter and she's a store clerk. We're not interested in the same things. She likes rock 'n' roll and things like that. She talks cat talk. I like, well, I'm more interested in . . . other things."

"Like getting into her pants?"

Dean's insides knotted. "Well . . . not exactly, I mean, I. . . ."

"Oh, then you're not interested in that?"

"Well, yes, but. . . ."

"But what?"

Dean shrugged with exasperation.

"But she wouldn't let you?" asked another detective.

"No. Yes, that's it. She teased, but didn't let me."

"She teased," said the second detective. "Well. I guess you got pretty riled up."

Dean heaved a deep sigh. "Sure I got riled up. Who wouldn't? You should see her."

"I may like what I see but I won't go scratching at her bedroom window."

There was a long, fan-zinging silence.

"Now," said the detective, "what were you thinking about? What made you go to her window? Why didn't you knock on her door?"

"Well, after I came home from drinking, she was waiting. She brought me in and fed me coffee and I made a play and she . . . she just wouldn't go for it."

"I see."

"I don't think you do," said Dean, "because there's more to it than that."

"Well, tell us. Tell us and we'll know."

"You see," said Dean, frowning, searching for the best way to phrase what he now felt forced to say, "she really wanted it. I mean, she got excited, more excited than I, if that's possible. But she just refused. She thought she'd be a nice girl by refusing."

"A nice girl. And what did you think of that?"

"She thought she'd be a nice girl so I'd think well of her. But, you see, I could never think of her the way she wants me to. She's nice—pretty, stacked, and all that. But we just don't see things alike."

"I see. I suppose you're a fellow with higher tastes," said the first detective testily.

"Well, damn it, what I mean is we come from different . . . different backgrounds. No, not backgrounds. We live in different . . . contexts."

"But you're not so highbrow that you wouldn't go sniffing around her window, even though she is intellectually beneath you. Is that it?"

"Yes, that's it. No, no it isn't. You make it sound criminal, but it isn't. I had hot pants for her and she had hot pants for me, and—"

"You thought you'd pay her a visit she wasn't expecting."

"Yes, that's it."

"I see." The detective wrote something on a notepad.

Dean felt a surge of indignation.

"Do you often go peeking in women's bedroom windows?"

"Of course not."

"Have you ever? You must have had hot pants before."

"No."

"Never?"

"Not never, but . . . I mean, sure I've peeked in windows. Who hasn't? But not the way you mean."

"The way I mean is, have you ever peeked into a woman's bedroom and thought about having the woman?"

"Well, good lord, who hasn't? Sure I've peeked into women's bedroom windows and thought of having some. And I've crawled in windows to get it. Who hasn't?"

"I, for one," said the detective. "I've always used the front door. But go on, continue."

"Continue?"

"Yes. Tell us about crawling in."

"Well, I don't think that's any of your business."

"Oh but it is."

"Look, you don't have to be a fiend to crawl through a window to see a woman, do you?"

"That depends on the circumstances."

"Well, it was by mutual agreement. She couldn't come out but I could come in through her window. So I did."

"My my! Why couldn't she come out?"

"Why?"

"Yes, why."

"Because, because. . . ."

"Yes?"

"Because she was married."

"Well. I see. But why didn't you use the door?"

"Because someone might have seen me going in."

"Hmm. Did you ever think of using the basement door?"

"There was no basement."

"Are you sure? Think back, now."

"Certainly I'm sure."

"Positive?"

"Yes. What are you driving at?"

"What do you think?"

"You mean the Donaldson murder?"

"You said that, not me."

"Well, is that it?"

"Is that what?"

"What you're driving at, what you're leading up to?"

"Now whatever gave you that idea?"

Dean huffed a sigh and slumped down on the stool again, slumped with his arms dangling between his legs, hands clasping each other tightly. He remained staring at his hands, relieved because he could see them clearly, in detail, fingers, wrists, nails, patches of hair; could see without straining against the glare of the overhead bulb. The shadows of the detectives on the floor around him were like members of an audience on the other side of stage footlights. Finally, he responded: "You can't think I had anything to do with that."

"Who said we did?"

"Well, do you?"

"Suppose," interceded the second detective, "we ask the questions, feller. Now let's just take this from the beginning. You were out on the fire escape peeking at a girl in her bedroom and you've done this sort of thing before."

"Wait a minute, wait a minute. That other was not the same."

"What kind of a window was it that you looked through? In that other case, I mean."

"Well, it was a, a, a window, that's all. Just an ordinary bedroom window."

"What kind of a house was this ordinary bedroom window in?"

"Look, that has nothing to do with—"

"Just answer the question."

"A one-story house."

"In town?"

"No, in a suburb."

"I see. And did you have to stand on anything to see into that other window?"

"Look, that other house wasn't—"

"Did you?"

"No."

"I see. And how did you enter the house?"

"I told you. Through the window."

"Was there a screen on that window?"

"No. Yes. Ah, hell, I don't remember. If there was, she took it out."

"I see. She was expecting you?"

"Certainly."

"And what did you do when you got inside the window?"

"What do you think?"

"Answer the question."

"I did what I came to do."

"Oh? And what was that?"

"That has nothing to do with this."

"Please, let us decide that, feller. Now, everything's going to be all right. You'll feel much better after you've told us everything and gotten it off your chest."

"But there's nothing to tell."

"Yes there is. What did you do once you got inside?"

"I went to bed with her, that's what."

"I see."

"No, you don't see."

"Now you say this house was in a suburb."

"Yes, in the suburb of another town."

"The suburb of another town? What town?"

"My hometown, Laughton. That's a small town at the other end of the state."

"I see. But you said it was a suburb."

"It is. Look on the map."

"I see. How long have you been a reporter for this, eh, this newspaper?" He nudged the floored *Chronicle* with the toe of his shoe.

"Couple of years. I handle the news in their town bureau."

"And how do you like being a reporter?"

"It's a job. The pay is bad, the hours are long, advertising is sold and the crud drifts to the top. It's a living."

"I see."

"No you don't."

"Please!"

"Pardon me," said Dean, sardonically.

"Anyway, to continue, did you cover the Donaldson murder?"

"Yes, I covered the Donaldson murder. Can't you read? That's my name over that sidebar story."

"Your name over a story doesn't necessarily mean you were there, does it?"

"Not necessarily, I guess, but I was."

"I see. Would you tell us about it? How you got there, how long you were there, what you did there, what you thought, when you left?"

"Well, I got the call at four o'clock and—"

"Four?"

"Yes, four."

"That's interesting. Who called you?"

"One of the neighbors. And I don't know which one."

"Is that a fact? Well now. I see. Go on."

"So, I jumped out of bed and went, that's all. I got there in about twenty minutes and just looked around, talked to Chief John and some of the detectives from the county and left."

"Left?"

"Yes, left. I went to change for work and have breakfast."

"Did you forget to get dressed when you went to the Donaldson home?"

"No, damn it, I didn't forget to get dressed. I threw on some old clothes."

"I see. What were you wearing?"

"Jeans and a teeshirt and a jacket."

"How about shoes?"

"Yes, shoes, too."

"I see. Which shoes?"

"Which shoes! Now how am I supposed to tell you which of my shoes I wore? A pair of shoes. Two shoes. Old shoes. No. Come to think of it, I wore boots, my hunting boots."

"And then you went to work?"

"And wrote the two stories."

"But while you were at the murder scene, what went through your mind?"

"Through my mind?"

"Yes."

"What am I supposed to do now? Remember every little impression that hit me and tell you about it and how I reacted to it?"

"Make it easy on yourself, son," said the first detective. "Just tell us what you remember thinking."

"What I remember thinking. Well, I remember thinking that the rediscovery of the century is that people are crazy. But I think that every day. And I remember thinking the road was unpaved, the house was eerie-looking, the auxiliary police were overly excited, the coroner is a slob. Oh, I didn't really think all that. I don't know what I thought. I felt more than I thought."

"What did you feel?"

"What do most people feel when they see a woman murdered?"

"What did you feel? You're a reporter: in your own words, what did you feel?"

"I told you what I felt in that sidebar story. I told everyone what I felt. Or, one version of what I felt."

The first detective groaned down to pick up the paper again. He read the story. The fan droned. The second detective stared at Dean. The third detective stared at his cigar. Dean pressed his hands together in an attempt to fight a fit of trembling.

The first detective dropped the paper again and said, "You ask, 'who is the maniac responsible?' Would it have to be a maniac?"

"Who else would do a thing like that?"

The three detectives were silent a moment, then the first said, "We found you on a fire escape about to break into a girl's bedroom. Are you a maniac?"

"No, but I had no intention of murdering her."

"No? What did you intend to do?"

"I, I, I don't know."

"I find it very interesting that you should write in the newspaper that you are wondering what maniac would do a thing like that to the Donaldson woman and then go crawling around on a fire escape trying to break into a girl's bedroom yourself. Very interesting. And yet, you don't consider yourself a maniac?"

"No. Look, you can't compare the two."

"Oh?"

"No, damn it! Being out on the fire escape—for me—I mean, I . . . that girl I was peeping at is my girl."

"But you said she wasn't your girl. You said you two just don't go together, that you're highbrow and she isn't."

"No, I didn't say it that way. I date her. I don't want to marry her, no. But I like her; she's my girl."

"She's your girl and you live in the same apartment house. Then why didn't you go to her door and knock, if you wanted to see her?"

Dean writhed with exasperation.

"You know," said the second detective, "you can make it a lot easier by telling us all about it."

"All about what?"

"All about what you intended to do when you were caught at the girl's window."

Dean froze into silence.

"Tell you what," said the first detective. "Suppose we give you some time to think it over. Suppose we leave you here alone awhile. Then when we come back, we'll see how you feel about telling us—about the girl and about that other time you went peeking into a woman's bedroom window."

Dean didn't answer. He sat with his head hanging, his arms drooping, staring at the brightly lighted floor between his feet. The three detectives left, quietly, almost on tip-toe, closing the door quietly, slowly, locking it.

Doubt springs eternal.

Quiet, you maniac!

Maniac!

Yes, maniac.

My friend, maniac is a harsh word for me. You were caught peeping in Sweet Reet's window. They want to know what you were doing there.

What I was doing there, yes. I was there, with you, Ally, to rape Sweet Reet.

Because Reet is rape-able. If not, you were to flee the scene, homeward bound.

Then some Peeping Tom spied a peeping tom.

Yes, the human predicament, conscience inverted, doubt in abeyance.

Doubt! You and your doubt. You mentioned storms and tidal waves, Ally, but you didn't mention police.

I quite forgot. But I was referring to the unknown when I was speaking of doubt, not to the conscience of a Peeping Tom peeking at a peeping tom.

Through a telescope.

It's quite laughable, when you stop to think about it.

Yes, Reet will say, when she learns of it— fun-nee.

So, laughing, here we are: peeping tom, intent to ravish, suspicion of murder.

The hell of it is . . .

Yes, it's true.

No.

Oh, but it certainly is. You did intend to ravish, if possible. Ravish was what you intended above all else. Ravish was what brought you out there. Ravish was what kept you out there.

No. You did.

You did, he did, they did, we did.

But when those idiots talk about it—

Yes, there is an unfortunate element of timing involved here.

Who do they think they are, anyway?

Police.

So what are police?

Morbid interest legally empowered to act, enforcing morbid interest.

But what do they want of me?

An answer: did you or did you?

Did I?

Not quite.

Could I?

Certainly.

Would I?

Maybe.

Sad, isn't it?

Very.

Could I, things being equally unequal, firm and unfirm, rape Reet?

Eue!

Would I rape Reet?

At least.

Hard to believe, isn't it?

No.

But, if I could and would rape Reet, does it necessarily follow that I could and would commit the other?

Luscious torso, legs akimbo?

No! Impossible! If this is possible, if I am capable, prone to such things—

Yes?

Who isn't?

Of the seedy set?

Yes, the seedy set.

No one.

Everyone?

Certainly.

The judge?

The jury.

The governor?

The hangman.

Everyone?

Everyone.

Shhh! There's trouble enough now, Ally.

Everyone.

They suspect the truth about my intentions.

They know it's possible for you because they know it's possible for them just as you know the other is possible for you.

No.

Oh yes.

But I wouldn't.

But you could.

But I didn't.

You came upon the scene and—

Saw the lady with the hatchet in her skull—
Saw her toes to nose, saw her bare, saw her
dead.

Felt the horror of it and—
And felt the delight in a glimmer, felt what
it would be like, tingled to the carnal sensation flickering.
But I didn't.
Didn't you?
How is it that if I admit to intentions toward
Reet, they'll suspect me of hatchet handling?
Skull smashing—
Those actions—
Those emotions—
That I could—
And maybe would—
But didn't—
Except. . . .
Oh yes, the dream.
And the thoughts, flickering.
But that's different.
In degree.
A great degree of difference.
The could from the would from the did—
by proxy.
But not really.
Really not factually.
Factually not really.
No, by proxy, by thought, by taste, by
feel, by sensation, inclination. By elation your relation to
sensation was the same as.
As what?
As why?
Why?
Because—
Because—

Because I saw her lying there on the cold basement floor
nude on the cold basement floor, lovely, and over the
horror of the fact washed the desire for the act, uncontrolled, it swept me under despite me, put the hatchet
in my hand so my palm dreamed the hatchet's
smooth wood pressing as the blade pulled its end
down and I felt my arm come up, then down,
then up, then down, then up to her dress and
pull and rip and tear her panties and bra, not
factually but really so that the emotions
and I merged into one and the same and
by proxy I became the killer as soon
as my eyes caressed her loveliness, her
dead inverted V and my lust rushed
in me but it hadn't left me and so
I dreamed it gushing to its target
and by dreaming and being and
knowing and feeling, I killed,
raped, for no reason ex-
cept unhinged desire, lust
out of control, lust on a
holiday with my need
making me the ma-
niac responsible—
not in fact, real-
ly, postmedita-
tedly I killed
her, raped
her, my me
in me did,
we did
we—
it &
I

Quite so.

Having experienced it but not done it—

Makes you guilty.

Guilty? No less than—

The doer.

No more than—

The viewer.

But they're looking for the doer.

They're looking for the one who held the hatchet, used the hatchet, ripped the clothes and raped the lady.

And I've felt—can now feel—the hatchet's wooden handle, its pressure against the heel of my hand, smooth, hard, pressed against the heel of my hand as I stand contemplating, pressed by the weight of the blade as it hangs down beside my leg; and now I feel my arm raise the hatchet, my hand tighten its grip, my arm flex for the act, throb for the act; and now I feel the flexed arm thrust, drive bounce and pull up to repeat; and now I hear the sound it makes— the whisper of parted darkness made by the flying blade, the solid bonks of the first few blows, the liquid smashes next; and now I feel my fingers slip between panties and skin and rip; and now, finally, I know through the darkness and on the concrete, I know what it is to have done it.

Guilty! You're as guilty as the grizzled, snooping coroner sniffing the corpse, as guilty as the carnal, bloodthirsty readers you entertained piously, as guilty as all who are capable of the act and as guilty as he who committed the act. Guilty!

As guilty as coquettish courthouse weavers of the hangman's rope, searching for the neck of a beast-doer who can be sacrificed to mollify the potential beast-doers?

Aye. Kill the guilty, spread his guilt thinly over the pious crust of finite order superimposed over infinite orderliness.

In the name of God?

No, in the name of guilt.

Human guilt?

Innate guilt.

Courthouse guilt?

Guilty guilt.

Pious guilt?

Pure guilt.

But, good lord, Ally, I didn't do it. I dreamed it and know it and heard it and smelled it and felt it, but I didn't *do* it. When did I become guilty?

At birth.

Then not alone.

Not alone in guilt, no. But now alone in the knowledge of guilt.

A difference. Please note the difference.

In degree. Always degree. Consider the doer: if his deranged mind is such that it convinces him he did nothing more heinous than drop a hydrogen bomb or hang a killer, is he guilty? If he feels, because of the strange sense of reality which infects him, that his act stemmed from and consummated something as pious as punishing the guilty to purge the innocent, is he guilty?

He's as guilty as I am.

As guilty as all are, but he doesn't know it so he might as well be innocent. If all knew guilt as you know guilt, as you *now* know guilt, who would be sacrificed to purge the sense of guilt?

Yes, who indeed?

So, only the knowers can stand up for the doers, can die for the pious.

Sacrifice myself? For them?

Bah! Such a word, *sacrifice*. Think of this: soon, humans being human, the man will push the button. All will go anyway, some way. And, the button being there and pushable, the finger being there to push it, it will be pushed. Boom.

But Christ! The sweet bloom of life is so sweet, sweet to the senses and sweet to the mind.

The flower that once has blown forever dies.

Omar-me not, Ally, not now. Not while I spin through this tunnel of madness.

We all have to go sometime, even the hang-men and button-pushers.

That's no consolation.

There is no consolation.

No, I suppose not. Sad, isn't it.

Very.

A laughable tragedy.

A sad comedy.

Thirteen men on a dead man's chest.

Yo ho ho and impending irony.

He heard the lock click, the door open, and saw the three detectives file back into the interrogation room. One carried a tape recorder. He lowered it gently to the bare, varnished hardwood floor near a wall socket, plugged in and laid the microphone nearby, but didn't turn it on. Then he joined the other two in a semicircle around Dean.

"Well?" said the first detective, "are you ready to tell us the truth about your activities for the past couple of days?"

"The truth? How will you know when I'm telling the truth?"

"It's our business to know."

"Ha! Your business!"

"Now, let's take it from the beginning again, from the time you were found on the fire escape. What were you planning to do?"

"Rape my next-door neighbor," Dean heard himself say. "I was planning to break in, turn out the light, and crawl in bed with her." The words tumbled out by themselves now, as if one of his selves had dissolved its will and another self spoke without interference.

The third detective quickly shuffled to the tape recorder and flipped the switch turning it on, then moved it closer to Dean and the others.

Dean continued: "I had to do something. The girl was driving me wild. I—"

The first detective interrupted: "What about the Donaldson woman? Was she driving you wild, too?"

"All right, damn it! Yes, sure, I'm guilty of that, too. As guilty as you and you and you, and all the others. Do you know what it's like to sink a hatchet into a woman's skull? Do you know what it feels like? I do. Think of it: how it feels in your hand, how your arm goes up and back then down. But you have thought of it, haven't you. That's your job, to think of these things. Then you know what it's like, and so do I, and I know that makes me as guilty as anyone— as you three and all the others."

"Now take it easy, feller," said the second detective. "Everything's going to be all right. Just take it from the beginning."

"From the beginning! In the beginning I was born. Then I found who I was, or who I thought I was; then I found that I shouldn't think of myself that way, that I should think of myself as others said they thought of themselves. Then I grew up, but I never could accept everything everybody else accepts—I mean, you're told things, tradition, history, this is a chair and that's a table; you are a man and she is a woman and you should behave according to such and such; and once in a while there's a war and you go to war and fight, kill the enemy because he'll kill you if you don't kill him, because he's been been convinced the thing to do is kill you just as you've been convinced the thing to do is kill him. So you kill. Then you come home and get a job and then the thing to do is be successful—get more for less, which is just about like war without sudden death. So you start out trying to get more for less, because you're told that's the thing to do. Everybody that's anybody has gotten more for less, either according to the rules or by beating the rules. But you can't quite get it through your thick skull that everybody's right, just because there's so many of them and only one of you. You wonder about the end of it all: the pit they'll lower you into, the heaven you're supposed to go to if you behave according to their standards. Then you think about their standards and come to the conclusion that it's all one big excuse for getting more for less, for killing slowly and surviving temporarily, for surviving temporarily in a manner thought of as successful. But you still can't get it through your thick skull that they are right about all those things and you are wrong in thinking it's all one big nuthouse. Then—"

"Wait a minute, wait a minute! Now, son," said the first detective sympathetically. But Dean, now approaching hysteria, blurted out:

"Give that tape to your hired psychologists. Let them hear it and smile knowingly and say my disorder is nothing new. No, nothing new. What I've said has been said before, they'll say, and they have a neat little cubbyhole, a scientific phrase to cover my problem. I can hear them now, rolling those musical Freudisms over their gums—problem stated. And as for a cure—"

"Just slow down, relax a minute," said the detective. "Take it easy. That's right, relax. Now, what we want you to tell us is how you went to the Donaldson home, how you entered and what you did there."

"Oh my God! What you want is for me to confess to rape and murder. And I've already told you I know what it's like, what it felt like. But you want more details. Okay. Turn up your damn tape recorder: here goes. I couldn't sleep. You know, it's been hot for spring, lately. So I got up, dressed in my old clothes and went to her house. But I parked down on the road so no one would see the car. Then I walked up that path through the woods behind her house, the one that

winds all around and finally comes out near her cellar door.
Then I forced open the door with the blade of the hatchet.
It's a loose door anyway; it wasn't hard to open. Then I
went into the cellar and called her name, softly at first, then
louder and louder, until I heard her stirring about upstairs.
She turned on the cellar light, but I wasn't afraid because I
saw I could knock it out or turn it off by unscrewing it. It's
just a bare bulb. Then I waited for her to come down the
stairs and she did, slowly, peering about, asking if anyone
was there. She saw the cellar door was open and, I guess,
decided to come on down and close it. When she got to the
bottom of the stairs and headed across the cellar floor to the
door, I jumped out from under the stairs and before she
could scream, I grabbed her and put my hand over her mouth.
But she struggled too much, so I had to hit her with the
hatchet and she fell, but she was only dazed, so I hit her
again with the blade and again and again and again, because
I knew now it was too late to do less. Then I smashed the
light bulb. Then I ripped her clothes off and raped her."

"Where did you get the hatchet?" asked the third detective.

"It's a boy scout hatchet. I've had it for years."

"Why did you go to the Donaldson home? Why there?
Why not to some other home?"

"Because I'd seen her. She works for the law firm next door
to my office. I've talked to her and knew where she lived."

"Why did she have her underclothes on at that hour of the
morning?"

"She hadn't been sleeping well. Had insomnia lately. I
guess she'd been up. She often got up in the middle of the
night and read. Ask the neighbors about that. They'll tell
you."

"You say you smashed the light bulb. How could you see
her in the dark?"

"Moonlight. Through the window. You see, I have all the
answers."

"Yes, you do," said the second detective.

"That ought to be a starter," said the third.

"Okay," said the first, "let's book him and can him."

The first detective, with a gentle pressure against Dean's back, persuaded him up from the stool, through the door and waiting room, to the desk sergeant's station.

"Charge him," said the second detective.

"Murder in the first degree," said the first.

"Him?" said the desk sergeant.

"Yup."

"All right. God, you never know. I never thought. . . ."

With one detective on either side of him, Dean was walked down the steps to the jail in the basement and locked in one of the cells. The only others in jail at the time were drunks, who moaned and gurgled and carried on sad monologues. The jail smelled of their presence—dank, putrid, like alcohol and urine and vomit mixed and aged.

The detectives left him. They walked out wordlessly. He discovered himself sitting on the steel shelf of a bed. Then he stretched out and went to sleep immediately.

He became aware of the scraping of feet over a concrete floor and thought momentarily that he was again watching the coroner and detectives in the basement of the Donaldson home. Then he heard laughter and excited voices and more scraping, and through his eyelids saw a brightness. He awoke to find himself blinded by a very bright light. He couldn't see past the light, but he heard the clank of the cell door and realized where he was. He sat up. Then, between his eyes and the blinding light, stepped a figure and he heard the desk sergeant's voice and felt his forearm touched by a hand.

"How about standing up, Dean," said the sergeant. "They want pictures for the television and the reporters want to ask you some questions."

Half from curiosity and surprise, and partly because the desk sergeant's voice was gently persuasive, Dean stood and faced the bright lights. The sergeant guided him by the arm toward the lights and soon he heard voices from the other side of the blinding barricade.

"Open the door a little, will you, Sarge?"

"Hey, Mac, that's my extension cord you're kicking."

"Wonder if we could have him outside the cell for just a minute, Sarge? Too much of a lighting problem when he's inside."

"Hey you, raise your hand over your head like you're holding a hatchet. Just for a second?"

"Sarge, how about pointing to him and looking at the camera. You know, about how you know him personally."

One of the bright lights went out momentarily while the cameraman stepped gingerly over the wires from the camera lights, shuffled into a new position to shoot from another angle and Dean caught a glimpse of several familiar faces. He saw good old Charlie holding his camera, waiting for the television boys to finish; Jim from the *Chronicle* and Ed Cory. Seeing Cory restored his stupefied senses and he realized, fully for the first time, what was happening.

Then someone stepped forward past the glare and he recognized Jack Wilson's voice. "All right, all right. How about breaking it for a little while, boys. I'm due on the air in twenty minutes."

There was a grumbled retort Dean didn't catch, then the bright lights went out, and he found himself confronted by a semicircle of television photographers and newspapermen. Wilson, with a tiny microphone in his palm, stood next to him, so close their shoulders rubbed.

"Dean? Is that your name?"

Dean nodded.

"What made you do it? Speak into this microphone, please."

"Do what?"

"Did you," asked Wilson, trying a different tack, "kill the Donaldson woman?"

"I did, you did, we did, they did," said Dean.

Wilson shot a significant glance to the desk sergeant, then asked, "When you went out for a drive that night, did you know where you were going? Did you intend to go to her house?"

Dean laughed a short "Ha!" Then he said, "No, Mr. Wilson, I really intended to go to church, but the church wasn't open so I went to her house, which isn't actually the same, but at least it was a place to go."

"I see," said Wilson. While Dean was speaking, Wilson had edged away from him slightly. "Would you tell us about it?"

"About what?" said Dean, beginning to derive a bitter enjoyment from the repartee.

"About what you did that night."

"Oh, that! Ah, you don't want to know about that. Too gory."

Wilson looked at the other reporters and shrugged. "How did you get into the house?"

"Which house?"

"The Donaldson home."

"Through the door. There was a tough doorman but I made it. I saw you and your mobile news unit outside. I was inside."

"Did you come up a nearby footpath? They found your footprints."

"Did they? Well, then I must have used the path."

"Then what did you do?"

"Sat on the cellar stairs."

"You went in and sat on the cellar stairs. Were you thinking about her?"

"Oh yes. Her and other things and other people."

"I see."

"You do?"

Wilson shrugged again, this time with more distinct signs of exasperation and disgust. "Then, after you sat for awhile, what did you do?"

"Got up."

"And. . . ."

"Stood."

"Then . . . ?"

"Walked around a little."

"In the cellar?"

"And upstairs."

"I see."

"You do?"

"Would you tell us, please, how you enticed Mrs. Donaldson into the cellar?"

"No. Trade secret."

"Eh, are you sorry about what you did, Dean?"

"I'm sleepy; I'm at least sleepy. I've been up since four A.M. today. Or was it yesterday? After only an hour's sleep."

"Do you have any regrets?"

"Yes, I regret your obnoxious presence."

"Would you have come in and confessed on your own if you hadn't been caught peeking in a girl's bedroom window?"

"Oh sure," said Dean. "Confessing's one of the easiest things in the world to do, once you get the hang of it."

"Have you ever been treated by a psychiatrist, Dean?"

"No, they've always figured I was beyond hope and treatment would be impractical. I never had much money."

"I see."

"No you don't."

"Did you know the Donaldson woman prior to the night of the murder?"

"Say, when was this murder? I thought it happened this morning. Or yesterday morning. Or, what time is it? Maybe it was this morning. No, it must have been yesterday. Hey, Mr. Wilson, it was yesterday. It's old news today. You'd better run along and find something new and exciting to chatter about. Aren't you a *news*man?"

"Did you know the Donaldson woman," persisted Wilson after a moment's pause, "before the morning of the murder?"

"I'd seen her, but she'd always had clothes on."

"Where did you see her?"

"Where *had* I *seen* her?"

Wilson frowned. "Yes, where had you seen her?"

"Nowhere. Everywhere. In my dreams and in my mind."

"Eh . . . then I take it you didn't know her personally?"

"How personal is personally?"

"I give up," snapped Wilson, stepping back into the ring of newsmen. "Didn't get a damn thing I can use, not one lousy sequence of sense."

"Well, he's not right," growled Cory. "I know. I talked to him this morning. He was pretending to cover the murder. But I smelled something wrong—I wondered how come he was there first, before me."

"No," said Jim, "he really does work for the Chronicle."

"He does? Really?" said Cory.

"He did," said Jim.

Wilson slid back to Dean's side and lifted the microphone to his lips. "After you killed the woman, you went back to the house and covered the story of it for the newspaper you work for?"

He shoved the microphone anxiously in front of Dean's mouth. "No. Before."

"What the hell," said Cory. "You see? He's nutty."

"He's bugs," said another.

"Okay," said the desk sergeant, "you guys have one more minute, then we'll have to close up shop for the morning."

Immediately the newspaper cameramen went into action. Dean winced at the bright flashes, and marveled at the pattern of tangled motion the photographers made as they stooped, sighted, stood and slid to another position, bumping into each other, oblivious of everything but their own activity. The reporters stepped back to give them more room and stood about placidly, hands in pockets or folded over their chests, waiting, watching Dean.

"Hey," Dean called to them, "you guys should be taking notes."

"Can't find anything about you worth noting," said one.

"My height, my weight, my appearance, my clothes. Better get all that straight so you all agree."

"Don't worry about it, chum," said another. "From now on, you won't have to worry about that."

"No, no more worries for me," said Dean. "I've already

done my worrying. Worried my way all the way here. You have a lot of worrying to do to catch up with me, chum."

"When you were very young," said a third, "did someone hit you on the head with a very heavy object?"

"Yeah, reality."

"Hey, this guy's a comic," said the fourth. "Hey, comic, did you enjoy using the hatchet on the lady?"

"As much as you did," said Dean. "Every bit as much."

A moment later, the cameramen finished with him and the sergeant led the dozen newsmen to the large sheet-steel door. They filed through one at a time. When they had left, Dean turned and walked back inside his cell and the sergeant locked the cell door.

"What time is it?" said Dean. He didn't really care. He just wanted to delay the sergeant.

"Eight, or a little after. My turn's over now and Depietroantonio's on the desk. If you want something, just rattle your cage. He'll come. They'll bring your breakfast about nine, after the traffic detail is done."

Then the desk sergeant walked away, picking his way carefully around the discarded paper cups, paper towels, old newspapers and other bits of trash which littered the jail floor.

The drunks had been turned out while Dean was sleeping. When the steel door clanked shut after the sergeant, Dean was left alone. He stretched out on the slab and tried to return to the dreamless sleep, but now his mind tumbled and spun to the rhythm of his subjugated anger, and . . . .

(MEAN DEAN, EUE DEAN, MEAN DEAN MEAN, and DEAN DEAN *are found sitting in committee on the rim of the cuspidor outside the cell door*)

EUE DEAN EUE
(*Dancing around them, holding a lock of Rita's hair between his thumb and forefinger, sings mincingly*)

A witch hunt, a witch hunt
We're going on a witch hunt
Hi de hi, hi de ho
We'll roast the cad, we'll make him glow
Honorable honorable is our name
By our rules is our game
Hi de hi, hi de ho
Come on gang, let's go!

DEAN DEAN
(*Rapping his gavel on the side of the cuspidor*)
Order, order! This meeting will not resume until order has been restored. Is that clear?

EUE DEAN
But Mister Chairman, we are in order, from left to right, and also in sequence, one through zero.

DEAN DEAN
Silence!

EUE DEAN EUE
But we are silent—utterly silent.

DEAN DEAN
All right. Now. The chair will entertain a motion from the floor—

SCRAP OF OLD NEWSPAPER
(*Lying on the jail floor*)
Vicious burglar killed by victim.

DEAN DEAN
—on the question which has come before this committee.

MEAN DEAN
I move—(EUE DEAN EUE *farts and giggles*)— that we suspend the regular order of business and recess to the hearing room,

and that we do there summon the subject of the recent debate
and question him directly about his strange actions.

MEAN DEAN MEAN

I second the motion.

DEAN DEAN

The motion has been made and seconded.

EUE DEAN EUE

Is there any toilet paper?

DEAN DEAN

Are there any questions on the motion?

EUE DEAN

If it please the chair, I wish to amend the motion as originally
stated. I wish to have included in the motion as it now reads
the stipulation that we do, after holding the hearing, impeach
the subject.

MEAN DEAN

Ah ha! Impeach.

EUE DEAN EUE

Yes, yes, impeach.

DEAN DEAN
(*Rapping gavel*)

Order, order! We now have a motion and an amendment to
that motion on the floor.

SCRAP OF OLD NEWSPAPER

Jazz mass packs church.

DEAN DEAN

Are there any further questions on either the motion or the amendment? If not, I'll call for a vote on the amendment. Those in favor of including the amendment with the motion?

EUE DEAN and EUE DEAN EUE
(Together, gleefully)

Aye!

DEAN DEAN

Those opposed?

MEAN DEAN and MEAN DEAN MEAN

Nay!

EUE DEAN

Hey, just a damn minute here! Mister Chairman, I object. I demand an explanation. The committeeman who seconded my motion to amend the motion has—

MEAN DEAN

I never!

MEAN DEAN MEAN

Neither did I ever!

EUE DEAN

—has dissented.

DEAN DEAN

So he has. That makes the amendment to the motion out of order.

EUE DEAN

Mister Chairman, I wish to go on record as objecting to the chair's ruling in this instance on the grounds that it is non-conforming.

DEAN DEAN

That is your privilege. Your objection is so noted. Now, is there any further question, or questions, on the motion to hold a hearing immediately? If not, I'll call for a vote on the original motion. All in favor?

ALL TOGETHER

Aye!

DEAN DEAN

Those opposed? (*From deep in the mire of the cuspidor comes a muffled groan*) Motion carried. Do I hear a motion to adjourn?

MEAN DEAN MEAN

I so move.

MEAN DEAN

I second the motion.

EUE DEAN

There he goes again, Mister Chairman.

DEAN DEAN

All in favor?

ALL TOGETHER

Aye!

DEAN DEAN

This meeting is now adjourned. As per previous agreement, we will now recess to the hearing room.

(*All rise solemnly from the rim of the cuspidor and move in an orderly procession through the cell door to the back of the cell where the hearing room has been set up. Bright spotlights illuminate the hearing*

*room; TV cameramen busy themselves. A press
table has been set up behind the cameras. The committee takes places.* DEAN DEAN *raps his gavel on the
cement floor.*)

DEAN DEAN

This hearing is now in session. We will skip the preliminaries,
with the committee's consent. (*All nod solemnly*) And get
to the witness. Will the bailiff call the first witness, please?

MORBID INTEREST

Will Mister President step forward, please?

EUE DEAN

With the chair's permission . . . ?

DEAN DEAN

Yes?

EUE DEAN

I would like to say I believe Mister President is asleep.

MEAN DEAN

Liar!

DEAN DEAN

You have, I suppose, evidence of a concrete nature to back
that statement?

EUE DEAN

I do, yes. Concrete and steel. It lies prone on that steel slab
in the back row in the unmistakable form of Mister President,
asleep.

DEAN DEAN

Ah yes. So it does. Bailiff, will you wake the witness, please?

MORBID INTEREST

With pleasure, Sir. (*He moves through the thronged hearing room to where* DEAN *dozes fitfully on the steel slab. He makes a fist and socks* DEAN *in the stomach*)

DEAN
(*Waking and gasping for air, holding his stomach, sitting up*)

Hey!

MORBID INTEREST

Will you step forward, please, Mister President. The committee respectfully requests your immediate presence.

DEAN

I, eh, I, well, sure, I guess so. Say, what is all this, anyway?

MORBID INTEREST

Perhaps, Mister President, you'll be able to enlighten us.

DEAN

Me? How? What have I to do with all this?

MORBID INTEREST
(*Seating* DEAN *at the witness table*)

That's precisely why this hearing is being held, Mister President.

DEAN DEAN

Will all rise, please? (*All do*) And now, our national anthem.
(*All except* DEAN *sing to the tune of* "America The Beautiful")

ALL

Cooperate, cooperate
Let each act for the good
Of employer and gadgetry
And tax collector, too.

(*Refrain*)

> Cooperate, cooperate
> Absurd to the absurd
> Oh question not
> The reason why
> God bless the FBI.

EUE DEAN
(*Carried away with patriotism, claps his hand over his heart and yells*)

Get the car with the go!

MEAN DEAN
(*Likewise carried away*)

Stop!

DEAN DEAN
(*Raps gavel; all respond by seating themselves again, then*)

And now, how does the accused plead?

DEAN

Accused of what?

DEAN DEAN

You know, do you not, the penalty for contempt?

DEAN

Contempt?

DEAN DEAN

How do you plead?

DEAN

Godless, I suppose. Yes, Godless, lost, beaten, adrift on an ocean of meaningless symbols, in a void.

EUE DEAN EUE

Eue Mister President, how pretentious and melodramatic you are today.

MEAN DEAN

Such a sweet smiling lamb with your ass in the teeth of catastrophe.

EUE DEAN

Do you see now, Mister President? Do you see now what you have done to the company, to the organization?

MEAN DEAN MEAN

Done, even though we told you so!

ALL TOGETHER

Yeah, told you so!

DEAN DEAN

Order! (*Raps gavel*) Mister President, I am, I must say, slightly taken aback by your strange plea—Godless. However, it is not the purpose of this committee to commit you or absolve you, one way or the other. We are simply here to determine why—why you so flagrantly and with no regard for your compatriots, allowed the company to crumble, to degenerate and disintegrate, to end up in jail, as it were, a confessor of guilt.

EUE DEAN

Mister Chairman!

DEAN DEAN

The chair recognizes Eue.

EUE DEAN

May I suggest we start from the beginning—or, that is, the beginning of the day, and approach the ultimate question chronologically?

MEAN DEAN
(*Sarcastically*)
One two three, tee hee hee.

DEAN DEAN
A suggestion is now before this committee. Discussion is in order.

MEAN DEAN
Mister Chairman, I see no reason to—

VOICE FROM THE GALLERY
There ain't no reason. It's the policy.

MEAN DEAN
—to go over this series of events in trivial detail—chronologically, as my esteemed colleague, Eue, proposes. May I propose another suggestion: that we waste no more time, that we crucify this faithless fool, this traitor, this maniac.

MEAN DEAN MEAN
Yes yes, crucify!

EUE DEAN EUE
(*Explodes with mirth*)
Tee hee hee! Haw! Ha ha ha ha....

DEAN DEAN
(*Raps gavel*)
Silence! Silence, you jackals! (*Pause*) Now. We have, gentlemen, two separate suggestions before this committee. However, I'm afraid the matter is one for the chair to decide. (*To himself*) After all, there comes a time when emotion must bow to the rules of procedure—principle and tradition. (*Addressing all again*) So, it is the decision of the chair that before action is taken, the witness will be given a full hearing.

(EUE DEAN, MEAN DEAN, EUE DEAN EUE, and MEAN DEAN
MEAN *moan loudly in agonized, frustrated protest*)

DEAN DEAN
(*Ignoring them*)
Now, Mister President, this committee, upon the inalienable
powers therein vested, does hereby demand a chronological
explanation.

EUE DEAN
Whoopee!

DEAN
Chronological? Well, I, I, I— Let's see. At four A.M.—

MEAN DEAN
You're forgetting something, Mister President.

DEAN
I said, at four A.M.—

MEAN DEAN MEAN
Of all the! Why don't you say it, damn you! Mister Chairman, I submit that the witness is uncooperative to the point of
contempt.

DEAN DEAN
Mister President, you do, do you not, know the penalty for
contempt?

DEAN
Well, but, you see, I, but. . . .

DEAN DEAN
Then you'll please confine your statements to those which
conform with traditional order as called for by this committee.

DEAN

Yes, Mister Chairman. (*To himself*) Seems to me that somewhere along the line, maybe while I was asleep, all the ground rules were changed.

DEAN DEAN

All right, proceed.

DEAN

Well, at four A.M.—

MEAN DEAN MEAN

There! Again he defies this committee, this organization, and thus he defies this great company. Mister Chairman, may I reiterate my previous suggestion—that the dirty, cowardly, traitorous son of a bitch be crucified immediately, crucified here and now until he doth be dead?

MEAN DEAN

Yippee! Cross your ankles, Mister President, so I can drive this nail through both your feet at once!

VOICE FROM THE GALLERY

Hey, wait. Just hang onto your kerchiefs a minute here.
(*All turn and lift their faces to see the source of the voice.* DEAN *recognizes the* OLD MAN *he met on the mountain*)

OLD MAN

(*As he makes his way cautiously down along the cement block side of the cell to the floor*)
Begging pardon, but you fellers is going about this thing all wrong. All wrong! In the first place, isn't Mister President entitled to a sidekick which whispers? And if that's so, I'm such a sidekick. And if him and you will be so good as to allow me, I figure to whisper.

DEAN DEAN

The committee resents this uncalled-for interruption, sir. You will kindly introduce yourself and—I might add—improve your smell.

OLD MAN

(*Now on the floor beside* DEAN)

The hell you say! With Kiddo's permission, I'll damn well whisper in his ear. Who I am and how I smell don't concern you fellers. Just you go on about your business same as before and I'll go on about mine.

DEAN

Old Man, I don't know what to do or say, except that you *do* need a deodorant.

OLD MAN

Shucks, Kiddo, ain't nothing but human you smell.

DEAN

Well, pull up a chair and have a seat, then. I'm ready to take anyone's advice on anything. Damn near.

OLD MAN

First, I got to say something. It ain't really worth saying, but I got to say it anyhow. Mostly just for fun, you understand. I got to say you fellers is still going about this thing all wrong. You ain't had this thing blessed yet. And you fellers know—or, that is, at least you think you know—that without a blessing this whole mess ain't worth diddly nothing.

DEAN DEAN

I'm inclined to agree with this, er, gentleman—in that one instance. We did, gentlemen, neglect the blessing.

OLD MAN

Well? Is he here?

THE BAR

I'm certainly heartened to find someone here has at last remembered the need to communicate with the Big Order prior to an undertaking of such vast significance as this one. Now, will the congregation rise, bow heads, clasp hands in front so that the arms form the rightside-up V.

(All do)

THE BAR
(Reads)

Blessed art they who believe in money, for they shalt be rich and poor.

Blessed art they who pay their bills, for theirs shalt be a credit rating.

Blessed art they who pay their premiums, for they shalt be insured.

Blessed art they who art married, for their couplings shalt be legal.

Blessed art they who pay their taxes, for they shalt build big bombs.

Blessed art they who build big bombs, for theirs shalt be interesting deformations.

Blessed art Old Dog Tray, for grief cannot drive him away.

OTHERS

Ahmen.

THE BAR

And now, the benediction. *(Sing-songing solemnly and making a big double X with his arm as he speaks)* In the name of the government . . . company . . . union . . . paycheck . . . Ahmen.

OTHERS

Ahmen.

THE BAR

Bless me Big O for I have thought.

OTHERS

Bless me Big O for I have thought.

THE BAR

Alle-gan-nee gannack, hoo ray. Ahmen.

OTHERS

Ahmen.
(*At this point, the music swells and the* PALLBEARERS *come upon the scene, trucking slow and cool in a return-from-the-cemetery strut, chanting to the tune of "When the Saints Go Marching In"*)

PALLBEARERS

We get still more
Still more for less
We get still more and more for less
We'll just keep right on getting
Getting still much more for less

THE BAR
(*When* PALLBEARERS *have finished and taken seats*)

Ah, yes, the chorus is in fine voice today, I see. Now, let us turn to page oh oh in the manual and lift our hearts in song to Big O.
(*Manuals rustle, all turn, sing*)

ALL

Big O love eue
Yes 'im do
For 'im pay eue
One twenty-two

Eue go downtown
Whoop-dee-doo
Back to Big O
One twenty-two
(*All return to their seats, snuggle into them contentedly,
and prepare to continue the hearing*)

DEAN DEAN

I'm sure everyone in this hearing room realizes the heartfelt thanks we all owe this old gentleman and I, for one, would like to offer the committee's. It indeed has done all our souls great good to have received his Reverend's blessing and to have lifted our voices in songed worship. Now, let's continue. Where were we?

EUE DEAN EUE

We were, Mister Chairman, on the verge of crossing Mister President's ankles.

DEAN DEAN

We were?

EUE DEAN EUE

We were. We, the committee, has come to the conclusion that Mister President is a scoffer, a sinner and, not only that, he ain't a sympathetic character.

DEAN DEAN

Committee? Might I have your word on this? I mean, of course, you understand, your collective word.

COMMITTEE
(*Chanting*)
Bump bump bump
His cross is dragging
Bump bump bump

He's mighty slow
Round the bend and up the hillside
On toward calvary we go

DEAN DEAN
Thank you, gentlemen. And now, Mister President, how do you plead?
(OLD MAN *whispers in* DEAN's *ear*)

DEAN
It don't make no difference, Mister Chairman.

DEAN DEAN
What?

DEAN
It don't mean a thing what I plead.

MEAN DEAN
Then cross your ankles, Mister President, so I can drive this nail through both your feet at once.

DEAN
Before I do that, I have one question.

DEAN DEAN
Yes?

DEAN
Do I have the right to summon co-witnesses?
(MEAN DEAN, EUE DEAN, MEAN DEAN MEAN, *and* EUE DEAN EUE *groan, scoff, boo, and hiss*)

DEAN DEAN
Co-witnesses? Hmm. (*Raps gavel*) Order, order! Silence, everyone! Now. Mister President has raised a point of order. How does the committee stand on this matter?
(*The others resume their noise*)

DEAN DEAN

Silence! I will rule. Mister President is correct in this matter.
He is entitled to call a co-witness.

MEAN DEAN

Since when?

DEAN DEAN

Since I so ruled, that's when.

MEAN DEAN
(*Derisively*)

He so rules! Get him! He so rules!

DEAN DEAN

Whom do you wish to call, Mister President?

DEAN

Sweet Reet.
          (*The committee as one sucks in its breath
          and falls silent*)

DEAN DEAN

Sweet Reet, please step forward.
          (*Down the aisle through the throng comes* RITA,
          *dressed for work behind the sales counter—high
          heels, tight skirt, sweater. The committee coos its
          enchantment.* RITA *walks up to the cell door and
          confronts* DEAN)

   You old silly, said Rita. What are you doing in there. Ah
Rita, said Dean. So glad you could come. Things were getting
out of hand here. That's why, said Rita, I had to see you
right away. I have something to tell you. I've talked to a
lawyer. Oh no, said Dean. Yes, said Rita. A good lawyer.
That's why I had to see you. The lawyer says to tell you he

can get you off with life imprisonment, and— Get me, said Dean, off with life imprisonment. What kind of *off* is that? Let me finish, said Rita, silly. He says to tell you that after, oh, treatments, oh, you know, that fun-nee word, like. . . . Psychiatric, said Dean. Yes, said Rita, that's the word. That funny word, said Dean. Yes, said Rita. Don't look at me like that. What's the matter. That, said Dean, funny word. Is that word a synonym for the castration of bronco sensitivities. What, said Rita. Nothing, said Dean. I'm trying, said Rita, to tell you what the lawyer says to do. Don't be such a smart alec. I don't have much time. I have to get back to the store or they'll dock me. Why, said Dean. Why what, said Rita. Why, said Dean, are you trying to help me. Well, said Rita, because you didn't do it. You couldn't possibly be the one, the maniac responsible. You were with me that night. Remember. Tee hee. Oh don't look at me like that or I'll slap your face. Go on, said Dean, tell me. Well, said Rita, then I went and got this lawyer and he says to tell you about the, oh, you know, treatments and getting out of jail and all. He thinks I'm a nut, said Dean. Well, said Rita, what else *can* he think. I told him you couldn't have done it, but in all the papers and the radio and all it says you confessed. Yes, said Dean, because I'm guilty. Eue, said Rita, that lawyer, he's right. No, said Dean, that lawyer is legal. I confessed because I'm guilty but I didn't do it. Don't run off, Rita. Hey, come back here. I'm not going to hurt you. What else did the lawyer say. He says, said Rita, to tell you he has a busy day in court and couldn't come to see you this morning but he may stop around this afternoon maybe. A busy, said Dean, day in court. Yes, said Rita, that's what he said. And he says to tell you you should be quiet and not answer any more questions until he comes and tells you what to say. Tells me, said Dean, what to say. Yes, said Rita. And he says for me to come see you and tell you because he has a busy day in court, like I said. Phew, it smells in here. Yes, said Dean, it does. Why, said Rita, don't they clean up and get rid of all this trash on the floor. Maybe, said Dean, they can't tell the trash from the floor. Tee hee, said Rita, don't be silly. How can you make jokes at a time like this. That, said Dean, is not a joke. Well, said Rita, don't look at me like that. And don't look at me that other way either. All right, said Dean, I won't look at you. What else did the lawyer say. He said, said Rita, to tell you what I told you. But what is all this about you being guilty, on the radio and in the newspapers and all. I tried, said Dean, to convey that I'm as guilty as anyone, or more so because I know it. Silly, said Rita, what made you say such an awful thing. You couldn't have done it because you were with me. He thinks, said Dean, that I put the hatchet in the woman's skull. Sure, said Rita, that's what he thinks. But I've got to go see him now and tell him that I saw you. I'm supposed to stop in and see him in court. See, he gave me the room number. See. Five oh seven. On the ground floor. Where, said Dean, the trash is. What, said Rita. Nothing, said Dean. What, said Rita, should I tell him. Tell him, said Dean, to forget it. What, said Rita. Tell him, said Dean, that if they ask me if I'm guilty, I'll say yes, and if they ask me if I did it, I'll say no. Tell him that. Eue Dean, said Rita, you're having a, a, a. . . . Nervous, said Dean, breakdown. Yes, said Rita, that's what you're having. And, said Dean, a nervous countdown. What, said Rita. Nothing, said Dean. Nothing at all. That's the way the cookie crumbles, is all. Please, said Rita, get some sleep. You look so, so, so bad and all in there. You were up last night drinking and up the night before, too. Remember the night before. Eue. And last night peeping. You were peeping at me, Dean. Eue. Why didn't you knock on my door. If you wanted to see me again, why didn't you just knock like a gentleman. I was only reading. I couldn't sleep either. You know I never read, except only to get to sleep. Yes, Sweet Reet, said Dean, but you're such a negative attraction. And when you curled up on the bedroom floor and started praying, that was too much. You, said Rita, tried to, to, to, well, you know what you tried to do. How many times must I tell you I'm a *nice* girl and don't do those things. How many. It's just, said Dean, that I don't like your ground rules. I suppose I don't have to let myself feel what I feel for you, but I don't see why I should prevent it. I feel it, so I feel it. That's, said Rita, only sex you feel. You're nasty. And that's why it's so dangerous, me living by myself without a roommate, because of men like you, nasty. I should have minded my own business and not even gone to that lawyer this morning. But before I go back to see him, I want to tell you something. If you hadn't been such a bad old silly, if you'd only acted like a gentleman— You'd have, said Dean, got me licensed. Eue, said Rita, don't talk like that. Stop smirking. I'm not, said Dean, smirking, I'm smiling. I shouldn't, said Rita, even tell you nothing. But I guess it doesn't make any difference now, since you're in there and I'm out here. So I'll tell you. Tee hee. What, said Dean, will you tell me. That, said Rita, I, I, I, wanted to marry you, that's what. Because I loved you, you old silly. You, said Dean, loved my old silly, so you wanted to marry it. Eue, said Rita, I'd like to brain you. And, said Dean, keep it from being silly. I, said Rita, should have kept my mouth shut. Yes, said Dean. Oh, said Rita, let's not part like this. Parting is such sweet sorrow. That's Shakespeare. I learned it in school. Anyway, I got to go now. The lawyer says to come right back and tell him. I, said Dean, see. Get the car with the go. Stop. Watch, said Rita, your language, I'm a nice girl. Have, said Dean, you always been a nice girl. Yes, said Rita. Well, except. . . . Except, said Dean, what. Except I had a crush on this here boy at home and, and, and. Yes, said Dean. And, said Rita, he ran off with this other girl from this other town. Hmm, said Dean, sounds familiar. And, said Rita, then Daddy died. Oh no, said Dean, not again. But, said Rita, I'm glad he ran off with the other girl. If I'd married him, I'd never have met you. But, but, but. Goodness. I got to go now. And see that lawyer. Don't, said Dean, forget what I said to tell him. I'll tell him, said Rita, you need a treatment. And some sleep.

Tell him, said Dean, I'm guilty but I didn't do it. What, said Scotty, guilty but you didn't do it. Yes, said Dean, that's just what I said. That, said Scotty, is not logical. Neither, said Dean, is it legal. I, said Scotty, just read your confession. Well, said Dean, how did you like it. Humph, said Scotty. We have four jails in this county and there's at least one confessor in each of them. That, said Dean, is encouraging. Encouraging, said Scotty. Is the whole world going nuts. I don't understand. What, said Dean, don't you understand. I, said Scotty, can see why some of those others confess. They're a special breed of psycho. But you, why did you confess. I, said Dean, am guilty. You, said Scotty, are sick. I, said Dean, didn't do it, commit the actual murder, put the hatchet in the woman's head, but I'm guilty just the same. I, said Scotty, repeat, you are sick. But we'll take care of that later. Right now, what I want you to do is repudiate your statement. I'll back you up, and I've talked to a girl who lives in your apartment building and she'll back you up, too. You couldn't possibly have done it. I, said Dean, know that. But can't you see that I'm guilty just the same. Like I said, said Scotty, we'll take care of that later. I'm sure it's nothing serious. Nor, said Dean, is it contagious. That, said Scotty, is a blessing. No, said Dean, it isn't. If it were contagious, don't you see what a difference it would make. Too much is contagious. Why can't this feeling of guilt and knowing it, why can't it be contagious. Like I said, said Scotty, you'll get the best the government can buy, the best specialists in the county. I, said Dean, don't want the best the government can buy. I don't want the best anything can buy. I want the best nothing can buy. If it can be bought, I don't want it. Whew, said Scotty, you sure have gone far out. No, said Dean, I suppose nobody can understand it. I, said Mark, understand. I understand completely. You, said Dean, understand that I'm guilty even though I didn't do it. Certainly, said Mark, but it's a thing you can't say logically or legally, scientifically or statistically, so you have trouble. Trying to say it is like trying to say where the squirrel cage we live in begins and ends. But, gather ye nuts while ye may, for soon thou shalt be put away. Well, said Dean, I'm glad someone can understand how it is with me, that I feel guilty, that I did it really enough, but not actually, that I know its doing from experience even though I didn't experience it. I feel better now. No matter what they decide to do with me, now I feel better. But, said Mark, since you can't get it across to them, you're in for a lot of trouble. Yes, said Dean, I know, and I don't relish the idea of being hung from the neck until dead. They, said Mark, won't do that. They're civilized. If they decide to kill you, they'll gas you. That, said Dean, that gas, that's what they don't use in wars, isn't it. Yes, said Mark, but you'll be inside a glass chamber, if they gas you, so there'll be no danger of wind blowing the gas back at the gassers. Of course the gassers get it in the end, too, but they don't like to think of it that way. They try damnably hard to convince themselves they will go to heaven and live forever, and that seems to make them better at killing. So it's gassers gassing gassers all the time, everybody going to heaven. Lovely chain reaction. I, said Dean, don't particularly like the idea of being gassed. Well, said Mark, you have choices, you know. You can repudiate your confession, or you can hire a lawyer, or you can stick to your story and get ruled insane. Well, said Dean, I can't repudiate my confession, it's a discovery I have to keep, even if they don't understand. And my guilt is not a thing which can be settled legally or logically. So I guess I'll have to stick to my story, my discovery, and let them rule me insane. Good, said Mark. You are so honest they will consider you downright stupid, and undoubtedly they'll rule you insane and have you committed. Well, said Dean, that's fitting. Committed for noncommittal. And, said Mark, for guilt. Yes, said Dean, committed for noncommittal and guilt. That's a perfectly fitting outcome.

The metal door groaned open and Dean was led from the cell by the desk sergeant. Before he was fully aware of what was going on, he was walking down a hall, up stairs, down another hall and then he was standing in the police chief's office. He slumped wearily into a chair at one end of the chief's desk, the chair he sat in so often while talking over news items with the chief. Behind the desk sat Chief Alex Dinkle; Scotty stood just inside the office doorway and Chief John, out of his jurisdiction for the occasion, leaned against a far wall. They stared at him intently until the desk sergeant left, closing the door.

Then Chief Alex cleared his throat and changed the expression on his face from frowning puzzlement to a mask of official confidence. They talked to him—in gentle tones, as to a sick friend. He listened unresponsively. Finally, they got to the point. He must promise to report to the county building and see the psychiatrist tomorrow morning at nine-thirty, and if he promised to do this, he'd be free to leave. Dean promised. Then he sighed and stood up. There seemed nothing more to say, no reason to stay. So he started to go.

At the door, Scotty detained him with a hand on his shoulder. "Don't worry, boy, it'll be okay. Talked to the girl who lives across the hall from you. She'll testify, if need be."

Dean opened his mouth to reply, but could think of nothing to say.

Then Chief John said, "Hey, don't you want to know if we caught the guy who did it?"

"No," said Dean.

"Another thing," continued Scotty, "we'll fix things up with the press. Have you all straightened out by the time the evening papers come out."

Dean laughed. Then he pushed past Scotty, through the door, down the hall past the desk sergeant and out. He took several deep breaths as he walked down the street with his torn shirt flapping against his back, his suit jacket over his arm, feeling a strange elation, a mad sense of comedy inside trying to come out. He had no words for it, had only the movement of himself along the pavement, around one corner, across the street, until he reached his apartment house. Then instead of going in and resting, he located his parked car. The keys were still in the ignition; in his excitement over Rita, he had left them there the night before. He got in and drove away.

He followed the route he had taken at four A.M. yesterday, out the highway to Swamp Run Road, out Swamp Run past the Donaldson home to the new highway up the mountain. It was deserted, both of traffic and road-building equipment, as it had been yesterday, and he gave vent to his mad elation by speeding. His foot went down hard on the accelerator; the speedometer climbed to seventy, then seventy-five, then eighty. The old car vibrated dangerously, but he kept his foot to the floor. When he came to the IMPROVED HIGHWAY AHEAD ROAD CLOSED UNDER CONSTRUCTION sign, he went straight at it, aiming his car at the center of the carpenter's horse from which the sign dangled. He growled a happy "Ah!" when he felt the impact, and chuckled loudly when he saw the sign and red lanterns hurtling through the air and felt the wheels of his car bumping over the long crossbeam of the carpenter's horse. He gazed at the wreckage through the rearview mirror and felt satisfied.

Then he noticed that his engine was overheating, so he slowed his speed as he continued up the mountain, enjoying like a child the climbs and plateaus. When he came to the vista which had caught his eye yesterday, he jammed on the brakes and skidded to a twisting stop in a short trail of sheared rubber—another satisfaction. He inspected the view for a moment, then with a whimper he heard before he realized he had uttered it, he squashed the accelerator again and went on, impatient with the car for sputtering and coughing, for not zooming off like a rocket. He drove with his teeth clenched, leaning forward against the slope of the rises, and in some deep-inside way, knew he wanted to keep on driving past the point where the new highway ended and became roadbed, on and on until his car could take him no farther; but at the bridge, he stopped. For there, down the slope from the road, sitting comfortably on a flat rock and waving to him, was the old man. He braked again, leaped out and scooped up a handful of stones and began throwing them at the old man, screaming curses as he did. But the old man never flinched; the stones flew wild, splashing into the stream, landing on the far bank. He stood still then, listening to the old man's cackled laughter; he returned to his car to turn off the ignition. Then, like a whipped dog coming home, he made his way down the slope to the old man, sat down on the bank a few feet from him and stared into the water.

"Make yourself t'home, Kiddo. Been expecting you," said the old man.

"Humph!"

"Yup. How'd you find jail?"

"Jesus Christ, old man, what the hell *are* you?"

"Not so good, jail, eh?"

Dean huffed with exasperation, calmed himself, and said, "No, not so good. But it looks like I'll be back."

"How's that, Kiddo?"

"I'm only out temporarily. They're going to examine me."

"How, Kiddo?"

"*How?*"

"Yeah, how're they gonna examine you?"

"Well, if I were a bug, they'd get a biologist to examine me. But I'm a man, so they'll use a psychiatrist."

"You gonna plead sanity?"

"No, *in*sanity."

"Yeah, that's what I mean—*in*sanity. Put the *in* on it. Won't believe you if you tell 'em the truth."

"That's right, old man. How'd you know?"

The old man cackled gayly. "Why, shucks, Kiddo, how I know is cause I don't. It's like the trout, them what got put in by the state and get pulled out by them what's sent up by the state to pull 'em out, the fishermen."

"Come on, make sense, old man. For a minute you were making sense. Don't talk riddles, make sense."

"I am making sense, Kiddo. So much sense it seems like *non*sense. That's cause of the hatchet just come out of your head."

"You know," said Dean, suddenly looking at the old man with wide-eyed fascination, "that's a strange thing. I think I see what you mean—about the hatchet. But unless I really am nuts, I don't have it in my head anymore. I pulled it out."

"Sure you did, Kiddo, sure you did. But you still got the wound. Take a little time to get over the wound."

"I see."

"Yup, I think you do. Now try to see the way it is with the trout—cause it's the same thing."

"There's the trout put in by the state," recited Dean, "and they get pulled out."

"That's it, Kiddo, and there's them what's on upstream, and they stay."

"Where are those trout, old man?"

"Oh you never seen them trout, them trout's *mine*."

"Now goddamn it, there you go again—you *own*, you *own*. You don't own a damn thing, old man."

"But I do, Kiddo, I do. And when your wound heals, you'll own, too."

Dean smiled wryly. "Afraid I won't be around, old man. Like I said, they'll examine me, then they'll hold a hearing and I'll plead insanity, and then they'll put me away."

"I know how it is, Kiddo. Soon's you get sane, they want to lock you up."

Dean looked into the old man's face suspiciously. "How do you *mean* that?"

"How? Like I said, same as with the trout."

"Oh Jesus, here we go again."

"Don't let your wound bother you, Kiddo. Just listen for a spell. It'll all come clear later. There's the trout the state stocks and there's them the state don't even know about, them which don't live in no state."

Dean lit a cigarette and blew a billow of smoke in a way to show his skepticism.

"*My* trout," said the old man, "live upstream. They swum and swum and swum to get there. It's a hard swim, getting up and outside the state, any state, all states. It's awful easy to go from one state to another, but it's hard to get out and stay away."

"I think I get what you mean, old man. I've been had, denatured, cut off, separated, lost. I've forgotten that I'm part of the grand scheme of things and so I lost myself in false, man-made things, things which don't really exist. Is that it?"

"That's a pretty highfalutin way to get at it, Kiddo, but you ain't there yet."

Dean pondered a moment, then said, "You're making a parable, then. You're saying it's hard to keep away from all forms and degrees of fanaticism and—"

"No no, Kiddo. Don't *use* them words. You narrow the stream too much, using them words. Just unthink it, wind out of it, and come at it the way I said, in fish and stream and state."

Dean lay back and rested his head and shoulders on a large mossy rock, and stared up past the trees at the sky. Seeing the treetops against the bare sky made him feel a sudden sense of tiny unimportance. People could destroy those trees, he said to himself, could destroy this mountain, all trees and all mountains, and still it would make no difference, except to people. He concentrated on the sight of the treetops against the sky, trying to hang on to this feeling of unimportance.

"Like them trees," said the old man in a whisper hardly audible over the whisper of the wind in the trees, "they ain't the state's neither, even if the state thinks they are. Them trees ain't got no hatchet in their skulls, and even if somebody comes along and puts a hatchet in their trunks, they still ain't the state's. No state's. Even if they get sliced up into lumber, they ain't."

"Whose are they?"

"They're mine, Kiddo, mine! They belong to my mountain and my sky. And all the hatchet-skulled states there can ever be won't never change that."

Dean blew smoke at the trees.

"And you can be like the trees, Kiddo, if you let yourself. Let that wound heal and then swim upstream, Kiddo. Swim so hard and far you leave all them states behind. Go so far, Kiddo, you ain't got words to say where you been and where you are. Go so far you ain't even got words like *fish* and *tree* and *stream* and *sky*, cause even them words can be hatchets, Kiddo."

Dean inspected his burning cigarette, then flicked it into the water and watched it float away in the current. "Old man, they may be about to lock me up in a nuthouse. If I go like you want me to, they'll never let me out."

"Naw, Kiddo, you ain't got it yet. I don't mean you should wiggle the handles of their hatchets and hurt them or upset them. When they say Buggaboo and expect you to say

Buggabah back, why shucks, Kiddo, say Buggabah. That way, they'll let you out."

"I see, old man, yes, I see."

"Sure you do, Kiddo, and once you're out, *then* you can start struggling past them hatchet-head words. *Then* you can go upstream, out of their states. And once you been here, Kiddo, you won't go back, no matter what words they use on you or you use on them. Then they can word you all they want and it won't make no difference, no difference. Then you'll see how nothing they ever do ever makes a bit of difference."

Dean stood and brushed off the seat of his trousers. "Okay, old man, I'll think about that. It'll give me something to think about in the asylum."

"You going there now, Kiddo?"

"Yeah, in a few days, maybe. First the examination, then the hearing, then the asylum. Maybe. And, like you said, old man, I'll give them Buggabah for Buggaboo so they'll think I'm in their state and let me go."

"Then," said the old man, "you'll come back up here."

"Yes," said Dean, "then I'll come back here and see how far upstream I can get."

The old man sat nodding his head in a contented old way as Dean left him and trudged up the slope to his car. On the road, he turned for a last look at the old man, who sat with his head cocked, smiling coyly. Dean didn't wave goodbye and neither did the old man.

Date

M
J

J